INFINITE KISS

A SWEETGUM MEADOWS ROMANCE BOOK 3

IMANI PRICE

First Edition: May 2023

ISBN 978-1-959039-78-5 (ebook)
ISBN 978-1-962071-93-2 (paperback)

Published by Books to Hook Publishing, LLC.
www.BooksToHook.com

CONTENTS

CHAPTER ONE

The setting sun cast a warm glow over the bustling city streets of Sweetgum, and Courtney relished the feeling of springtime in the air. April was always a magical month, full of hope and renewal. As she walked briskly from work to the book club at Rochelle's Diner, she smiled at the thought catching up with her friends.

Despite the beauty of the season, Courtney's day had been exhausting. Her job at the cell-phone store was a never-ending cycle of mindless sales pitches and rude customers. The lack of opportunity for advancement, along with the monotony of it all grated on her nerves. It was a far cry from the life she had envisioned for herself after college, but she couldn't deny that it paid the bills.

Courtney also did tax preparation, but it was only a seasonal gig at the beginning of the year. In addition to that, she had a steady income from balancing the books at the town hall and offices once a month. It was a simple and boring task, but it paid the bills. Joanne had offered her a job at Roasted Beans Coffee Spot, but Courtney knew she needed her own thing. She was determined to find a job that fulfilled her and made her feel truly alive.

After college, she had explored various career paths, but sales had always been her specialty. She had discovered her talent for it during a local scout troop's cookie sale drive when she was just eight years old. But now, as she approached the diner, she wondered if there was more to life than just making sales and balancing books. This is something she'd been thinking a lot about lately, and she was determined to find a way to get the fulfillment she sought.

She was grateful for her supportive friends and family, but she knew that ultimately, she had to figure out her own path in life. She sighed, pushing the thoughts away, and focused on the present moment.

As she pushed open the door to the diner, the sound of excited chatter and the aroma of freshly brewed coffee greeted her. She smiled to herself, looking forward to a night of engaging discussion and companionship with her fellow book club members.

Courtney was very involved in the lives of her friends; the recent development between one of her best friends, Brandi, and the love of her life, Chris, warmed her to the bone. It was so adorably beautiful, their earnest love of shared interests and each other lighting a fire under Courtney. What was she even doing with her life? She had to consider these questions, man or not. She wasn't eager to just jump into a relationship, but she had to consider where her life was heading as she hadn't figured it all out just yet.

The warm glow of the setting sun filtered through the windows of Rochelle's Diner, casting a golden light over the patrons enjoying their meals. Courtney felt a sense of contentment as she entered the diner and was greeted by the excited chatter of her book club friends. The aroma of freshly brewed coffee mingled with the scent of warm muffins and made her stomach growl.

"Hey, Courtney! Over here!" Joanne called out, waving from the corner booth. Courtney made her way over to her friends, smiling at their excited chatter. She slid into the booth, feeling the plush cushion of the seat envelop her tired body.

"Hey guys, how's it going?" she asked, rubbing her eyes. "Long day at work."

Kim smiled at her sympathetically. "I know the feeling. I've been trying to wrap up everything before my trip with Malik," she said, gesturing to her boyfriend, who was sitting next to her. "I had to make sure all my braid clients knew that I wouldn't be available. We're leaving next week for New England and then heading west to explore some national parks."

"That sounds amazing," Courtney said, feeling a twinge of envy. "I wish I could take a break like that."

Malik grinned. "You should! Life's too short to spend all your time working."

Courtney nodded, feeling a pang of guilt. She knew she needed to find a job that fulfilled her and made her feel truly alive, but the thought of leaving her stable job made her nervous since she didn't have a backup plan.

"Anyway," Kim said, interrupting her thoughts. "Let's get started on the book. What did you guys think of the sheriff?"

As they delved into an animated discussion of the latest romantic comedy, Courtney felt a sense of gratitude for her friends. They were always there for her through the good times and the bad. She made a mental note to take Malik's advice and start exploring new opportunities.

Courtney took a sip of her coffee and settled back into her chair, eager to hear what her fellow book club members thought of the latest read. The book was a romantic comedy featuring a charming small-town sheriff in Wisconsin, and she couldn't wait to hear everyone's opinions.

"So, what did you all think of the book?" Rochelle asked, leaning forward on the edge of her seat.

"I loved it!" Joanne exclaimed, clasping her hands together. "It was such a heartwarming story, and I couldn't put it down."

Kim nodded in agreement. "I thought it was a really fun read. The characters were relatable, and the romance was just the right amount of cheesy."

"I have to say, I was pleasantly surprised," Brandi chimed in. "I'm not usually one for rom-coms, but this one had me hooked from the first chapter."

Malik chuckled. "I have to admit, I wasn't sure what to expect when Kim suggested we read a romance novel, but I have to say, I enjoyed it. The small-town setting and the sheriff's character were really well done."

Courtney nodded, a small smile on her face. "I agree. I thought the author did a great job of bringing the setting to life. I could almost smell the fresh air and feel the warmth of the sun on my skin."

Rochelle grinned. "Well, it sounds like we all enjoyed the book. So, any thoughts on what we should read next?"

Courtney looked around the table and realized that her friend Nevaeh, who had been uncharacteristically quiet, had yet to share her thoughts on the book. "Nevaeh, what did you think of the book?" she asked, turning to her friend.

Nevaeh looked up, a thoughtful expression on her face. "Honestly, I didn't enjoy it as much as the rest of you did," she admitted. "I mean, it was well-written and all, but I just couldn't get into the whole small-town sheriff thing. It felt a little too cliché for me."

There was a moment of silence as the rest of the group processed Nevaeh's opinion. Courtney could see that Rochelle was about to say something, but before she could speak, Joanne jumped in. "Hey, everyone's entitled to their own opinion, right?" she said with a shrug. "I thought it was great, but I can see why it might not be for everyone."

Kim nodded in agreement. "Yeah, I think it's important to have diverse opinions in the book club. It makes for more interesting discussions."

Rochelle nodded, a smile on her face. "Absolutely. So, Nevaeh, do you have any suggestions for our next book?"

Nevaeh's face brightened, and she reached into her bag, pulling out a well-worn copy of a classic novel. "Actually, I was thinking we could read this," she said, placing the book on the table.

Courtney leaned over to get a better look at the cover and smiled. She had read that book in high school and had loved it. She could already tell that this was going to be a great choice for their next read. She settled back into her chair, feeling thankful for her friends and the stimulating discussions that always left her feeling inspired and fulfilled.

The group chattered cheerfully, tossing out titles and authors left and right. Courtney listened with interest, taking mental notes on the books that sounded intriguing. She loved being a part of this group, and she appreciated the opportunity to discuss literature with such a diverse and intelligent group of people. It was nights like these that made her forget about the monotony of her day job and reminded her of the joy that could be found in the simple things in life.

As Courtney indulged in the delicious meal, her mind drifted, and she started to feel a nagging sense of restlessness. Her mind was consumed with the question that had been weighing on her for weeks - what was she doing with her life? Despite Rochelle's impeccable hosting skills, Courtney found herself distracted, lost in her own thoughts. Before she knew it, the evening was coming to an end, and only Courtney, Joanne, Neveah, and Rochelle were remaining.

"Hey, you've been in your head all night," Neveah spoke, gaining Courtney's attention. "What's going on?"

"I hate my job," she sighed, pinching the bridge of her nose before adjusting her long gray and black dress.

Neveah let out a heavy sigh, her fingers delicately adjusting Courtney's necklace as she offered a warm smile. Joanne and Rochelle watched on, their expressions brimming with concern. It was clear that something was troubling their friend, and they were eager to hear what was on her mind.

Courtney took a deep breath and opened up to them, pouring out her thoughts and feelings over the course of the next hour. The discussion touched on everything from her job to the direction of her life as a whole. It was a serious brainstorming session among some of the smartest and most insightful women that Courtney knew, and by the end of it, she felt renewed and inspired. This wasn't a pitiful, sobbing mess of a revelation – it was a cathartic moment of growth and introspection, thanks to the unwavering support of her closest friends.

"She's a hell of a saleswoman, she really is," Rochelle said, pushing her long braids, compliments of Kim, over her shoulder.

"She could sell the desert some sand," Joanne agreed, playfully nudging her as her curls bounced with laughter.

"Okay, so what is it she could do that gives her some sort of boost to rediscover her passions?" Neveah asked, gently pushing her hair from her face. "There has to be something you could do with your paintings, Court…."

Courtney hesitated for a moment, biting her lip as she considered Neveah's words. She knew deep down that she had a talent for painting, but the practical side of her brain always held her back. "I don't know," she admitted, her voice laced with insecurity. "It's not like I can make a living off of painting. I can't just quit my job and pursue it full-time."

Joanne reached over and gave her hand a reassuring squeeze. "Maybe not full-time, but you can still make time for it. You don't have to give up your job to pursue your passion."

Brandi nodded in agreement, her eyes warm and supportive. "And who knows? Maybe you could make a living off of it. You won't know until you try."

"She needs a man," Rochelle smirked, sounding like the resident matchmaker that she was, but the three of their eyes went wide. "What?!"

"First," Courtney began, crossing her arms defensively. "I don't need a man to be happy or fulfilled."

"No, no," Joanne sighed, trying to redirect the conversation. "It's not about what you need; it's about what you want. It doesn't have to be a man, but about what inspires your passions, Court."

"I understand what you're saying, but why would a man want me if I can't even have passion for my job?"

"That's ridiculous!" Neveah interjected, stopping them all with a hand. "Why wouldn't a man want you? You're the prize, Court; I know you don't usually have a problem with self-esteem, so where is this coming from? You shouldn't think like that. Look at Kim and Brandi!"

"What about them?" Courtney asked, shaking her head so her hair bounced. "Just because they found love doesn't mean we all will…."

"Ouch," Rochelle sighed, shaking her head. "You definitely need something…."

"I've got to get home," Courtney shrugged, standing from the booth. "Doctor's appointment in the morning."

"You okay?" Neveah asked, her eyes growing wide.

"It's just a routine checkup I've put off for too long," she said, reaching out to hug her. "I'll see you guys later."

"Good night!" Joanne called after her, offering her a hug as well before she left the mostly empty diner. It was late and she had to walk back to her car parked at the cell phone store. Courtney was relieved that the parking lot lights had finally been fixed and drove the five minutes across town to her small apartment complex.

Courtney lay in bed, staring up at the ceiling, her mind consumed with the question of what she wanted in life. Her friends had made some valid points at the book club meeting, and she couldn't shake off the feeling that something was missing. She had been so focused on her job and her daily routine that she had forgotten about her passion for painting.

As she lay there, contemplating her future, the idea of finding a man crossed her mind. It wasn't the main focus, but it was something to consider. Maybe a partner could help her find the inspiration she needed or just provide some companionship in this dull life.

She pondered the thought of dating apps, but the idea made her cringe. Instead, she decided to focus on rediscovering her passions and exploring new avenues in her life. If a man came along, she would be open to it, but she wasn't going to actively pursue it.

With a sense of determination, she closed her eyes and made a mental note to start painting again.

THE NEXT MORNING, Courtney woke up once again, feeling restless and dissatisfied. She tossed and turned throughout the night, her mind consumed with thoughts of what she really wanted to do with her life. As she sat in front of her tablet, scrolling through social media and various websites, she couldn't shake the feeling of emptiness that had settled in her chest.

Despite feeling lost, Courtney knew she had a doctor's appointment to attend in a few hours, so she forced herself to get dressed. As she stood in front of her closet, she thought about the conversation with her friends the night before. The part about the possibility of finding love.

As she got dressed, she thought about all the romantic books and television series she had consumed over the years and how they had given her a false sense of what love and happiness looked like. She knew deep down that she needed to figure out what she wanted for herself and not just what society told her she should want.

Shaking herself from her stupor, Courtney headed to her doctor's appointment at a practice near Sweetgum Hospital. On the way, she stopped by Joanne's café, Roasted Beans Coffee Spot, to get some extra motivation. The café was packed with familiar faces. She was also happy to see that Joanne had found more permanent help since she offered Courtney the job a few months ago.

After the coffee and a drive over to her appointment, Courtney felt like the day was already dragging. The appointment was unremarkable; the older woman talked to her about her stress level, mental health, and her general well-being before giving her a clean bill of health. She was relieved, having a curious flu a couple of weeks ago. Now that she was finished at her appointment and on her way to work, Courtney let her mind wander once more.

The position of an assistant manager at a phone store that dealt with pre-paid and contract phones wasn't exactly the dream job that she had envisioned for herself. However, it did have some perks, such as flexibility and full-time benefits. But that was no longer enough.

As she drove through the familiar streets of Sweetgum, Courtney thought about her parent's divorce. It was an event that had shaped her life, but she didn't like to dwell on it. She remembered the arguments, the tears, and the feeling of being caught in the middle. But she also remembered the moments of peace and love that followed when her parents put aside their differences to make sure she was okay. Despite this, Courtney couldn't shake the feeling that love was fragile, that it could be taken away at any moment. It made her cautious in matters of the heart, always looking for the catch, the flaw that would inevitably lead to heartbreak.

As Courtney drove through the winding streets of Sweetgum, she felt a sense of pride in her family's deep roots in the town. Her great-grandfather's great-grandfather was one of the town's founding fathers, and she loved hearing stories about his determination and grit. She cherished the old watch that had been passed down through the generations, an heirloom that had survived time and turmoil. As she ran her fingers over its intricate design, she smiled at the memories it held. She had salvaged it from the chaos of her parent's divorce, a tangible reminder of her family's resilience and strength. The watch was now securely fastened around her neck, a precious treasure she always carried with her.

Courtney's fingers reached for the watch around her neck, her heart warming at the thought of its history. She remembered her father telling her the story of his great-grandfather's grandfather, his journey from New Orleans to Georgia after the Civil War, and the scattering of their family. It was a tale that had captivated her as a child and one that she held dear to her heart. She took the watch out from under her square-neck tunic and examined it. Over a hundred years old, the antique timepiece had been the first item her great-great-grandfather had purchased with his own money. She ran her fingers over the engraved casing and opened it to check the time, even though she knew it was already displayed on her car's dashboard.

The polished silver watch had always been a comfort to her, with its thick glass face and intricate clockwork mechanism. She would often find herself lost in thought, gazing at its face and feeling a sense of calm wash over her. However, as she drove down Main Street that morning, she was jolted out of her reverie when she saw that the watch had stopped. Her worst fear had come true, and she felt a sudden wave of panic wash over her. She checked the time again, listening closely for the ticking of the clockwork, but there was nothing but silence. She felt a moment of panic, the weight of anxiety overwhelming her. As she approached the only major intersection on Main Street, she felt a sense of dread wash over her. But as she rolled through the intersection, she saw a sign in the distance that caught her eye.

She spotted the small storefront wedged between Rochelle's Diner and Mrs. Zhang's Chinese restaurant, with a colorful sign hanging above the door that read "Justin Time's Clock and Watch Repair."

With a glimmer of hope, she pulled into the nearest parking spot and hurried inside. She stepped through the door, the tinkling of a bell signaled her arrival.

CHAPTER TWO

*J*ustin bounded down the stairs of his shop with a grin on his face, eager to start working on his latest custom watch for a repeat customer all the way from Japan. As he brewed a fresh pot of coffee in the back of the shop, he felt a sense of contentment wash over him. He was excited to get started on the day's work, and he felt confident that his unique, vintage-inspired designs were just what his customers were looking for. His outfit of choice for the day was a suit, not because he thought it made him look professional but simply because he liked the way it made him feel.

As Justin made his way to the back of the shop, he navigated through the maze of tools and equipment scattered around the room. The smell of sawdust and chemicals filled his nostrils as he passed by a table piled high with wooden gears and intricate pieces waiting to be assembled into a custom clock. On the left side of the room, he could see his soldering equipment, still hot from the last repair job he had done. The woodwork area was on the right, with various stains and finishes sitting on a nearby shelf.

Despite the apparent chaos, everything had its place in

Justin's workshop. He knew exactly where to find each tool when he needed it, and the sight of the various pieces of machinery brought a smile to his face. As he walked past a shelf lined with grandfather clock faces, he ran his fingers over the smooth surfaces, admiring the craftsmanship that went into each one. For Justin, the workshop was a sanctuary, a place where he could lose himself in the art of clockmaking.

The narrow yet deep brick-faced building that housed the shop was a part of the historic downtown area, untouched for the past 150 years. It had been a general store before becoming a watch shop, and before that, it was the first sundries shop in the area. The interior was steeped in history, with crown molding and plaster carvings adorning the ceiling. The most remarkable feature was the beautifully restored chandelier made of copper and bronze, illuminating the shop with a warm glow.

Justin stood in the middle of his workshop, surrounded by the tools and equipment of his trade. He picked up a soldering iron and examined it closely, admiring the way the light reflected off the smooth metal surface. The scent of chemicals and wood chips lingered in the air, a familiar scent that made him feel at home.

Just as Justin was about to pick up his tools and get to work, his phone rang, interrupting his peaceful moment. He frowned, recognizing the number of his ex-wife. She had been trying to reach him for weeks, ever since her relationship with her new guy had ended.

"Hello?" Justin answered, his voice curt.

"Hey, Justin, it's me," his ex-wife Maureen said, her voice sweet and apologetic. "I know I messed up, but I still love you. Can we talk about getting back together?"

Justin rolled his eyes, feeling the anger boiling up inside him. "No, we can't," he said firmly. "I'm done with this. I'm done with you calling me every time things don't work out with some guy. You cheated on me, remember? You destroyed our marriage."

"I know, I know," she said, her tone now pleading. "I was young and didn't know what I wanted, then. But I promise I've changed. I realize now how much you mean to me."

Justin shook his head, not believing a word of it. He hung up the phone, feeling even more irritated than before. The thought crossed his mind that he should block her, but for some reason, he just hadn't done it yet.

He didn't trust women anymore, not after what his ex-wife had done to him. He didn't need anyone in his life, he thought. He had his work, and that was enough.

But as he picked up his tools and began working on the custom watch, he wondered if there was someone out there who could change his mind. Someone who could make him believe in love again. He pushed the thought aside, focusing on the intricate mechanics of the watch. Love was the last thing he needed right now. People lied, and love hurt.

After his divorce, Justin had spent months soul-searching and trying to find his place in the world. He had dabbled in various hobbies, from hiking to painting, but nothing had given him the sense of fulfillment that working with watches and clocks did.

As he looked around his workshop, he felt a sense of pride in what he had built. The brick storefront that housed his shop and apartment was a symbol of his hard work and dedication. And the small, historic house he had purchased last year was his latest project. He had thrown himself into the renovation with gusto, spending countless hours sanding, painting, and repairing.

As he stood there, lost in thought, he began to consider his options for the house. Should he move in and make it his home? Or should he flip it and use the profits to invest in his business? The decision weighed heavily on him, but he was confident he would make the right choice. After all, he had found his passion in life, and he was determined to make it his career.

The morning light spilled through the windows of Justin's workshop, casting a warm glow across his workbench. He carefully inspected the custom clock he had just finished for his Japanese buyer, admiring the intricate details that he had poured so much of himself into. As he was lost in thought, the bell above the door jingled, signaling the arrival of a customer. Justin looked up to see Mrs. Baker, one of the regulars, shuffling in with a worn wooden clock in her hands.

"Good morning, Mrs. Baker," Justin greeted her warmly. "What can I do for you today?"

"Well, my old clock here has been acting up, and I was hoping you could take a look at it," she explained, setting the clock down gently on the workbench.

Justin smiled reassuringly. "Of course, let me take a look." He carefully opened up the clock, his nimble fingers quickly identifying the issue. He set to work, tinkering with the delicate gears and mechanisms until the clock was ticking steadily once again.

As he finished up the repair, Mrs. Baker peered over his shoulder, her face creased with curiosity. "How do you do it?" she asked, watching his skilled hands with wonder.

Justin chuckled, setting down his tools. "It's all just a matter of understanding how these old mechanisms work. I find it fascinating, really."

And he did. As he returned the clock to Mrs. Baker, he felt a sense of satisfaction at the thought of restoring something so cherished to its former glory. While custom orders were exciting, there was a certain charm to the small repairs that kept him rooted in Sweetgum.

His next customer of the day didn't come in until after ten, inquiring about a repair for his high-end smartwatch valued at several thousand dollars. Of course, Justin was happy to help, but it wasn't exactly his passion. All watches were unique and beautiful, but he didn't care much for the new smartwatches and digital versions. It took the art of watchmaking and basically threw it in the garbage, though his strong opinions might not be too popular. After the customer left, intent on leaving his smart watch for repairs and cleaning, Justin grabbed another cup of coffee, settling into his worktable just inside the workshop door. He could still see the shop and the front door from here, eager to grab his magnifying glasses and lamp to see what could be wrong with the smartwatch in question.

He was only ten minutes into investigating when the front door chime rang again. Another customer was almost welcome, but when he looked up from his desk, he was immediately struck. He would normally greet a customer enthusiastically, but this particular customer had stunned him. She was wearing a beautiful flowing tunic of pale green and black fitted jeans, her bright eyes alight under her beautiful, natural curls. Her smile was slight yet genuine when she spotted him, but something danced behind her expression that concerned him. When she approached the small counter, he sprang up, feeling like an idiot for being struck by the woman.

He noticed the way her eyes sparkled and the way her hair fell in soft curls around her face. He had never felt this kind of response before, not even when he met his ex-wife. He couldn't deny that there was something about her that drew him in, but he quickly reminded himself that he needed to keep his distance.

As he stood there, trying to maintain his composure, Justin felt a sense of danger emanating from this woman. He knew it was irrational, but his instant attraction to her felt like a threat.

"Hello," she smiled, unclasping her necklace. "You are probably really busy, but do you do custom repairs?"

He forced a professional smile and greeted her with a curt nod, hoping to keep their interaction strictly business. He didn't want to encourage any sort of personal connection, especially with someone he had just met.

"Absolutely. What can I help you with?" he asked curtly.

"I've got this pocket watch, and it is a family heirloom," she said, showing him the silver piece.

He couldn't help but be a bit shocked, reaching to take it from her and inspect it closer. It was a custom-made, old watch with cogs, wheels, and pieces from the late 19th century. It was fascinating examining its silver, bronze, and wooden aspects. He could sense both anticipation and worry in her as he inspected it with his magnifying glasses and a small light.

"It is a beautiful piece," he told her as he inspected it with his magnifying glasses and a small light. "Crafted sometime in the late 19th century, it's made of real silver and bronze, with some wooden pieces that add beautiful detailing. Is there a story behind it?" Justin asked, examining it more closely. "And forgive me, I didn't catch your name, Miss...?"

Courtney smiled, extending her hand. "Oh, please, my name is Courtney Mathews. You're Justin, yes?" she inquired.

"That's correct," Justin replied, his tone cool and distant. He took her hand briefly and released it, not bothering with a smile. "Justin Clark, at your service."

"Oh, I should have known the name of the shop was a fun pun," she laughed.

Justin forced a polite smile, though his tone remained formal. "Yes, it is." He felt a tingle run down his spine as she leaned closer, invading his personal space. He tried to subtly edge back, but she continued to hover over the counter.

"And the watch has such a long history. It'd take all afternoon to tell you. I don't suppose it is an easy fix. So, what's the verdict, doc? Will it live?" she asked, still leaning in.

Justin forced a tight-lipped smile and nodded. "It's a delicate piece," he said curtly. "I'll do my best to repair it, but I can't make any promises. It may take some time to find the right parts and get it working again."

Courtney's smile faltered slightly at his response, but she pushed forward. "I understand," she said, trying to keep the disappointment out of her voice. "I just really need it fixed. It's been in my family for generations."

"I won't lie, it is a very old piece, with custom settings and specific-sized cogs that just aren't made anymore," Justin said roughly, staring back down at the silver pocket watch. He had been avoiding eye contact with Courtney since she walked in, afraid of giving away his feelings. "I don't want to get your hopes up, Courtney…"

"Please, if there is anything you can do, money is not a problem; I just need it fixed," she pleaded, her voice trembling with emotion. Her eyes shone with an intense fervor that was impossible to ignore. Justin felt a surge of empathy towards her and nodded, removing his glasses.

He met her gaze directly, trying to hide the flutter in his heart. "I will try my best to repair it." He knew he was acting immaturely and had to suck it up and do his job. "Also, I would love to learn about the history of this piece. It's truly unique and unlike anything I've seen before."

"I'd love to tell you the story," she said with a slight smile, "but unfortunately, I have a job that keeps me busy during the weekdays. Would it be possible to schedule a time for us to meet over the weekend?"

"Of course," he replied. He knew he couldn't get too close to her, but he was extremely attracted to her. "I'll be here and available for you."

Why did I say that? he thought to himself. He had to get his head on straight. "Also, if I manage to find a solution before then, I'll give you a call. For now, would you mind filling out this ledger for me? It's a standard procedure for our records and invoicing."

Justin handed Courtney a folder containing some intake paperwork that he needed her to fill out, including her consent for him to take the watch apart and continue with the repairs. He watched as she filled out the paperwork, unwillingly impressed with her perfect penmanship. While he wasn't sure what he could accomplish with this piece, he was willing to give it a try. He was drawn to her love for the watch, and he wanted to learn more about her, even though he was hesitant to get too close.

"There we are," she said, handing over the completed ledger. "I put my email, home phone, cellphone, and work phone, in case."

"Thank you, Courtney. This is thorough." Justin said, looking over the completed paperwork.

"Thank *you*, Justin," she said. "I was sad when I saw it had stopped. I've been very careful to wind it and maintain it, but I guess it just couldn't keep going forever."

"I understand," he said, carefully placing the watch on the work surface of his desk before turning back to her. "It's natural for these old watches to stop eventually, but don't worry, I'll do my best to bring it back to life."

"Thank you so much," she sighed, glancing at her phone as it buzzed. "Oh, I'm running late…"

"Don't worry, I've got this," he assured her, grabbing the booklet with her contact information from the counter. He wanted to see her again, but he knew he had to keep his distance. "And I'll be in touch as soon as I have an update."

"I really appreciate it," she said gratefully, waving goodbye as she hurried out the door. Justin watched her go, feeling a sense of confusion at his conflicting emotions as a sense of relief washed over him when the bell above the door signaled her departure.

CHAPTER THREE

*C*ourtney sat behind her desk, watching her sales staff as they busied themselves with organizing a new wave of phones for display. But despite the flurry of activity around her, she couldn't shake the building tension inside of her. Her thoughts kept drifting back to the antique pocket watch she had left with Justin two days before.

She had been debating whether to reach out to him. Part of her worried she was being too pushy, but the other part was desperate for any news about the watch. She had been keeping herself busy with work, but deep down, she knew it wasn't really that busy—just inventory and pushing the recent sale.

As she thought about the watch, her mind kept wandering, unable to shake off the lingering thoughts of the handsome store owner. She wondered if Justin could fix the watch, despite his warning that it might not be possible. But there was something else that kept nagging at her, something she couldn't quite put her finger on. Ever since she had met him, there had been a growing sense of eagerness within her, which was confusing and unexpected.

When Justin first saw her, he was polite but distant, and she felt like he didn't want to be bothered. But as they talked about the watch, he seemed to warm up to her.

Courtney felt confused about the mixed signals Justin had given her. On one hand, he had been warm and understanding, meeting her gaze directly and conveying both his empathy and determination to help. On the other hand, she sensed a distance in him, as if he was holding back or hiding something. It was frustrating, especially since she couldn't tell if it was related to her or if he was just naturally aloof.

She had replayed their conversation over and over in her head, trying to find clues. Did he feel the same attraction she did? Was he just being friendly and professional? She didn't know, and it was driving her crazy.

"You okay if I take my lunch now?" one of her employees asked, breaking her out of her reverie, a young man with a sharp haircut and a dazzling smile.

"Oh, yeah, go for it. I'll go after you," Courtney nodded, then turned to the college girl flirting with him. "You can do lunch after me, okay?"

"Sure thing," the girl smiled, waving after the young man as he grabbed his jacket and cell phone from the back room.

Courtney's eyes wandered around the store as she tried to keep her mind occupied. The same old faces came and went, all looking for a good deal. She smiled politely at each of them, but her heart was not in it. She longed for something more fulfilling, something that would challenge her and make her feel alive. She remembered how she used to enjoy selling things, getting the customer just what they needed, and watching their satisfaction. But now, it all seemed so mundane, so unexciting.

When she started working here four years ago as a part-timer, it was just to earn some extra money in school. But now, as the assistant manager of the store, she felt trapped. Her manager rarely came in, leaving her to deal with the day-to-day operations of the store. She yearned for something more exciting, something that would reignite her passion for selling.

Her phone rang. Her manager's voice sounded tired and distant. "Hey, I'm not going to be able to come in today," he said.

She took a frustrated breath. "I can't keep doing your job, you know. You can't just keep calling in sick every other day."

"I know, I know. I'm sorry, but I've got this really bad migraine and I just can't get out of bed."

She resisted the urge to roll her eyes. "Look, I've got two other employees to oversee, and I'm only the assistant manager. It's not fair that I have to keep doing your job."

"I know, I know. I'm really sorry. But can't you just handle things for today? I promise I'll make it up to you."

"No, I can't. You need to come in and do your job. I can't keep doing this for you."

He sighed heavily on the other end of the line. "Okay, okay, I'll try to make it in tomorrow. Just try to manage things for today, okay?"

She hung up the phone feeling frustrated. She knew that she couldn't keep letting him walk all over her and take advantage of her hard work. This was getting so old and she was so over it.

Courtney leaned back in her chair, lost in thought about how she'd let things get this far out of hand. The sound of the door opening and closing drew her attention, and she looked up to see her employee sauntering in, grinning from ear to ear, still buzzing from his usual lunch of an energy drink and jerky. She rolled her eyes at his antics, but was secretly grateful for the distraction.

The store fell quiet except for the murmur of the two young employees chatting and laughing in the corner. Courtney stole a glance at the clock and realized it was almost one. She sighed and got up, preparing to take her own lunch break.

"I'll be back in an hour; try not to burn the place down," she smiled, grabbing her bag and jacket.

"Have a good lunch," they both smiled, waving after her.

As Courtney left the store for lunch, she adjusted her knee-length business skirt. Her white button-up shirt was tucked in neatly, giving her a polished appearance. She wore a black belt with a simple metal buckle that added a touch of sophistication to her outfit. Despite her desire to maintain a professional appearance, her long, curly hair had a mind of its own, bouncing freely with each step she took.

Courtney's mind was set on checking in at Justin Time, hoping for an update on her watch. She walked a couple of blocks up the street towards the shop. The door chimed as she entered the store, but there was no sign of Justin. Courtney wondered where he could have gone, but her curiosity was quickly overshadowed by the stunning displays in the shop.

She had been too anxious to notice the beauty surrounding her during her first visit. But now, the vintage watches, the delicate clockworks, and the intricate trinkets were all too captivating for her to focus on anything else. She wandered around the shop, admiring the craftsmanship and unique design of each item, completely lost in her thoughts.

As she stepped deeper inside, the scent of wood and polished metal filled her nostrils. The narrow room was lined with tall shelves, each crammed with a hodgepodge of items - watches, clocks, antique jewelry, tarnished silverware, and even a few old books. The light filtered in through the small, dust-covered windowpanes, casting an ethereal glow across the shop. Courtney's eyes darted across the room, taking in the stunning display case in the center. Inside, she saw an array of intricate items - pocket watches with delicate filigree, ornate brooches, and even a few antique pistols.

Despite growing up in this town, she couldn't believe she had never stepped inside before. Every inch of the store was crammed with fascinating objects, each with its own unique story to tell.

The thought that Justin might design and create the pieces himself finally struck her, and she paused, her eyes scanning the intricate details of the watches and clocks in the shop. Could it be possible that he was a true craftsman, not just a seller? The watches looked like no others she had seen before, and the wooden clocks were absolutely gorgeous, with a modern yet antique style. She was admiring a particularly unique piece on the shelf when she heard a noise. She jumped, turning toward it to see Justin smiling in the doorway of his workshop.

"So sorry to interrupt," he said, smiling kindly at her through his short dark beard. "You like?"

"It's beautiful," she sighed, staring back at the piece.

"Thanks," he shrugged, glancing at the back room. "I was just working on a repair and had planned on shooting you an email today about your piece."

"That's why I'm here," she stated, still looking at the shelves. "Did you design all of these?"

"I've designed and created most of them," he nodded, his voice tight all of a sudden, becoming distant. *There he goes with all those mixed signals*, she thought.

"I don't mean to interrupt," she said, as she approached the counter. She was determined to get this watch fixed, even if that meant going somewhere else. She hated to doubt his skills, but it seemed like he didn't have much confidence about it when she dropped it off. She knew she had to temper her expectations.

"You're not interrupting," he assured, his voice still tight. "I don't mean be short with you. I'm just a straight talker."

"I see, but it's always good to be at least a little pleasant when working in sales," she chided, which surprisingly caused a smile to spread over his face.

"Noted. Is that what you do? Sales?"

"I do, at the cellphone store," she said. "Not my passion, but I guess I'm still searching for my calling."

"That's honest," he said, leaning casually against the counter now. "Busy morning at work, then?"

"Big sale," she smirked, rolling her eyes. "But I didn't come to talk about my job…."

"Oh, you didn't?" he joked, a twinkle in his eye.

"I was wondering about my watch," she laughed, leaning against the counter as well. "I couldn't think about anything else, and I was wondering… What I mean is… were you able to do anything?"

CHAPTER FOUR

$\mathcal{J}$ustin hated the idea of crushing her optimism. She was so happy and excited and seemed a bit afraid, which made all of this worse. He didn't know what to do because he had exhausted all his resources, and nothing had come of it. The piece was beautiful, uniquely built, customized, and absolutely impossible to find parts for.

"I've got to be honest; I feel like an absolute jerk for having to tell you this but…."

"Oh, no," she replied, her eyes falling immediately.

"I'm sorry, I really am, but I've contacted all my contacts, suppliers, historians, and just about everyone I can think of," he replied, reaching out to comfort her but stopping himself. He didn't want to be forward and honestly had no idea what he was trying to do. "I mean, it is a rare specimen. The maker, back in the 1890s, was only in business for three years and custom-made all his watches. He was known for them, actually…."

"Really?" she asked, her eyes going wide again, but this time with wonder.

"Well, yeah, he's a lot like me in that sense," he chuckled, admiring her unabashed curiosity and eye for creativity. The guilt inside him was turning and coupled with the anxiety of talking to a beautiful woman, made him blurt out the first thing he could think of.

"I have an idea," he said, meeting her gaze confidently. "I could try building the necessary parts myself to fix the watch."

"Really? You… you'd do that? I mean, it's possible?"

"It's possible, as I've made many customized pieces," he said, his smile spreading as he scratched his beard nervously. "I've got the tools to make custom pieces, but I've never tried to make something like this, recreating a historical piece."

"I don't want to get in the way of other orders," she insisted. "But, the truth of the matter is, I really need to get this watch fixed."

"The thing is, the original parts are simply not available, as they were custom to only a few watches, and it would take me a long time to really delve into it."

"I understand that it'll take time, and I'm willing to wait if you're willing to fix it," she said.

"I am. Here, let me bring it out and I'll show you want I mean so we can both be on the same page."

He returned with the watch and its deconstructed broken pieces on a small work surface he had, setting it down on the counter to show her. She was so excited, coming around the counter and staring over his shoulder closely. He was a bit nervous about her being so close, but he continued, explaining each broken part, essentially what it did, and part of the process of recreating the pieces. She took it all in, listening closely and asking all sorts of questions. She seemed so different from his ex-wife, who never took an interest in anything he did. But people lie and she could just be acting to get what she wanted.

"So, this one interacts with the cog that turns the bigger hand," she said softly, leaning close. "And it is so small. You can recreate it for real?"

"For real," he said, reminding himself that people could be

manipulative and she could be trying to butter him up to get him to fix the watch.

"Oh, thank you so much, Justin!" she smiled, bobbing on the spot before wrapping her arms around him in a hug.

It caught him completely off guard, but she seemed not to notice, her smile wide as she let go and stared back at the watch pieces. He could feel the heat on his face but refused to acknowledge it, turning back to the piece as well.

"Thank you," she repeated, her smile so wide he reflected it back at her. She stayed there another ten minutes as he explained a few signature markings on the watch. Then, when her phone buzzed, she groaned, realizing what time it was.

"That'd be work," she sighed, smiling weakly at him. "Back to the store. I hope to stop in again if that's not too annoying."

"Not at all; stop in whenever," he encouraged, unable to stop himself as she walked back around the counter.

"Really?" Courtney asked, her bright eyes alight. "I'll take you up on that offer, Justin."

"Please do," he smiled, once again speaking before he actually had time to think. He could see her cheeks slightly flushing, his own body responding with a slight increase in heart rate.

"I want to help in any way I can as a thank you," she said, turning from him. "And I would love to explore this shop some more. I am ashamed to say I've never been in here until this week."

"It's a shame; it's a great historical piece of Sweetgum," he said solemnly, shaking his head at her, causing her to chuckle.

"I work again tomorrow, but how about the day after? I can come in and help out a little with the customers if you show me what to do?" she asked, his heart skipping a beat.

"Sounds like a plan," he nodded, watching her leave with a smile on her face and a spring in her step.

When she left, he immediately exhaled equally curious and confused about the beautifully vibrant and snappy woman he'd just met. His mind was racing, their chemistry obvious to even him, as jaded as he felt. He was so nervous, anxiety rising, until he had to take a minute and sit back down in his office.

Focusing on the piece in front of him and working on the smartwatch he wanted to return tomorrow, he fell into a groove. He preferred to work alone, to not open himself up to judgment, criticism, or pain, but with what he'd just agreed to with Courtney, that was impossible now. It startled him to find that he cared what Courtney thought of him already. That scared him more than the daunting task of repairing that irreparable watch. Something inside him was shifting, and he had to stop it, his hands becoming unsteady until finally, he needed to just call it a night.

She was on his mind as he closed up, took the piece upstairs to store in his vault, and contemplated dinner. He just wanted to order in, ignore his thoughts, and be content again like he had been before she arrived. It was impossible. The curve of her smile, the trill of her voice, and the vibrance of her eyes were absolutely undeniable. It was dangerous and he couldn't handle it.

His divorce a couple years ago was messy, his feelings crushed when his ex-wife left. She had been sleeping with her boss for months before they finally separated, his heart broken and irreparable, like the watch. It was his own choice, refusing to feel pain like that again, but as all the good stories told him— real bravery was to get back on the horse.

Perhaps that was a bit cheesy, but he'd been hesitant to even approach the horse. It wasn't like he'd planned this meeting with Courtney, or her beauty both inside and out. She was something different, something genuine, her feelings and emotions right on her sleeve for all to see. It was a huge change from the illusive and deceptive experience of his ex. They'd been together for years and all he kept thinking the whole divorce was who else did she cheat on him with. He hated how insecure he had become when he was with his ex. He felt that he wasn't enough for her, that she had to go outside of their marriage. He felt like a failure, like it was his fault.

He'd been deeply hurt and couldn't gloss it over like it was nothing. Sure, it would have been convenient to just get over it like people insisted upon. It'd be nice if he could just do that without any issues, but sadly he had that monster in the back of his mind, whispering lies and fears into his ear. This time it was no different, the fear and anticipation of Courtney returning overwhelming him the rest of the night and into the morning.

CHAPTER FIVE

ourtney was tired of complaining about how her life wasn't going the way she wanted, so she decided to do something about it. She loved painting above all, how had she forgotten that and why had she thrown it to the side? She was feeling inspired and had the overwhelming urge to express herself through her art. So, she stayed up all night, painting her emotions onto the canvas in the abstract style she adored. As she painted, she felt a sense of release, as if the colors and lines were taking her on a journey of self-discovery.

As she worked, she became more and more engrossed in the process. She mixed different shades of paint together to create the perfect color for each stroke of the brush. She made long, sweeping motions with the brush, letting her emotions guide her hand.

As the night wore on, the painting began to take shape. The maze of lines and shapes started to make sense, and the woman in the center became more defined. She was sitting in a meditative pose as if she had found the clarity and inner peace that Courtney was searching for.

Finally, as the first rays of dawn peeked through her

window, Courtney put down her brush and stepped back to admire her work. The painting was a true representation of her journey, and she felt a sense of relief wash over her. She knew that the road ahead wouldn't be easy, but she had taken the first step toward finding her true self.

⁂

"You look like you could use some espresso," Joanne smiled, sliding down onto the couch next to her.

Courtney had come into Roasted Beans Coffee Spot early that morning, far too early. She was so deep into her thoughts that Courtney hadn't noticed Joanne grab them both another latte with a single shot of espresso. When she came back to the couch, and Courtney was still lost in her thoughts, Joanne smirked, clearing her throat. It wasn't until that moment that Courtney looked up, her cheeks flushing with embarrassment.

"Latte for your thoughts?" Joanne asked, handing her the simple mug. "You're so out of it this morning."

"I'm just thinking," she admitted, staring down into the delicious-smelling cup of Columbian roast. "My watch, the one that's been in my family for generations, broke."

"Oh, Court…"

"I took it to the repair shop, you know?" she nodded, sipping on the steaming hot cup. "Have you ever been in there?"

"No, I haven't, actually. But, I've met the owner, Justin, being that his shop is right up the street," Joanne shrugged, leaning back against the couch comfortably. It was one of those lucky mornings where the shop wasn't too busy, her two baristas easily handling the dozen-or-so customers they'd had in the past hour.

"It's really interesting," Courtney admitted, cradling her cup in her palm as she leaned over her crossed legs. "It's like a museum, antique shop, and repair shop all wrapped into one."

"I'm going to have to tell my granny," Joanne smirked, nudging her friend. "She's been looking for a mantle clock for quite some time."

"Oh, she'll find it there, I'm sure," she nodded, smoothing the long sundress she'd decided to wear that day. The forecast had predicted lots of sunshine and Courtney was going to take advantage.

"So, what did Justin say about the watch?" Joanne pressed, taking a sip from her cup.

"Oh, right. So, he took a look at it and when I came back for his assessment, it was a bit disappointing," she admitted, pushing some of the loose curls back behind her ear again.

"What kind of disappointing?"

"Well, he said the parts for the piece are simply not made anymore," she nodded, staring out the window now. "He said he contacted his manufacturers, suppliers, and even his antique collectors and nothing."

"I'm so sorry; what will you do with the watch then?"

"Oh, Justin still has it," Courtney said, sipping from her steaming mug again. "He said he could try and recreate the parts himself."

"Really?" Joanne asked, her bright eyes wide. There was something behind those eyes; Courtney watched her warily.

"It's a lot of extra work, so I agreed to help him out around the shop and deal with customers," she responded. "He's been kind for the most part, so I had to do something to help him out other than pay for the work itself."

"Uh-huh." Joanne winked, while Courtney shifted uncomfortably and avoided making eye contact.

"Stop it!"

"You stop it," Joanne laughed, flipping her hair over her shoulder. "So, tell me about Justin…."

"You're impossible!" Courtney giggled, shaking her head at her friend, who clearly knew what she was thinking.

"You like him," Joanne smirked, wiggling her eyebrows suggestively. "So, go for it!"

"I don't even know him," Courtney protested, taking a drink from her mug. "We're perfect strangers."

"Then get to know him," Joanne insisted, setting her mug down. "Seriously! You might find that you have a lot in common."

"Like what?" Courtney scoffed, still holding her mug. "What do I even say? Hi Justin, I'm a part-time manager at the cell store in town and do tax prep and accounting in my spare time. That just sounds appealing, doesn't it?"

The sarcasm in her voice was thick, Joanne's brow furrowing with concern as Courtney sipped on her mug of hot coffee again. There was a silence; Courtney feeling annoyed at first, but now it was fading into hopelessness, something Joanne seemed to notice immediately. She hugged her gently now, her arms squeezing her tightly as the two sat on the comfortable café couch.

"Sorry," Courtney finally said, her head hung low. "I'm just not in the right headspace to think about anything like that."

"Is it that bad?" Joanne questioned, still holding her close with one arm.

"Being an accounting major is probably the worse idea I've ever had," Courtney grumbled, setting her mug back down. "I mean, I'm grateful for the work at the town hall every month and the business of tax season, but I absolutely hate everything about it."

"Hate?"

"Hate!" she groaned, pinching the bridge of her nose before smoothing her pale sundress. "I honestly wish I never chose that major. Like, I only cared about it because it was something steady, financially stable. Everyone needs an accountant or tax prep!"

"Everyone needs coffee, in my opinion," Joanne smirked, nudging her to try and get a smile.

"See, and you love coffee. You love having your own business and dealing with your customers," Courtney smiled, leaning against Joanne's shoulder. "But I'm so miserable and it's becoming more and more obvious as time just drags on. I'm wishing I would have gone with the art degree instead."

"Awe, Court, I had no idea you were that miserable," Joanne sighed, squeezing her tightly. "What can I do?"

"Nothing, really," she whispered, watching the growing traffic outside the window as the small town hummed to life. "I don't know why I didn't choose something that I was passionate about. I love painting, but I was too worried about money. I would rather be poor and happy than rich and miserable."

"You're not rich now, my love," Joanne smirked, desperately trying to get her to smile. "But I know what you are saying."

"I'm so lost right now, and I have no idea what I'm doing," Courtney grumbled, grabbing up her cup again to take another sip.

Joanne was about to respond when the large group of older women, who formed what the town liked to refer to as the "hit and run" squad, entered with their matching tracksuits. Courtney knew many of them from book club, but the two baristas were swamped immediately, Joanne jumping up to help. Courtney didn't mind her friend leaving their conversation, watching her face light up when she greeted everyone. Joanne knew their orders right away before the older women actually spoke them. She was happy to talk and laugh as the other two baristas started helping her with the first three drinks.

As she sat sipping her coffee, Courtney admired how much Justin seemed to love his job. She had watched as he tinkered with the gears and cogs of the watch, his eyes sparkling with excitement as he talked about the different mechanisms. It was clear that he had a passion for his work, something that Courtney longed for in her own career.

She thought back to Joanne and how she always seemed so fulfilled in her job. As she looked around the cozy coffee shop, filled with happy customers and the warm aroma of freshly brewed coffee, she wondered if it was time for a change. Even her friend Brandi, who worked as the head teacher at the local daycare, seemed to love her job.

Courtney took another sip of her coffee and let out a heavy sigh. Maybe it was time for her to take a leap of faith and pursue a career that brought her joy and fulfillment.

CHAPTER SIX

Another quiet morning had come as Justin stretched in his large bed. The smell of his coffee brewing in the other room was always a motivator, the sun not quite up over the horizon yet. It was still dark, hazy, and completely quiet, the time of day he enjoyed most. As he stood from his bed and peered out his bedroom window at Main Street below, Justin wondered if it would be a good day.

He didn't dwell on it, slipping into the bathroom to get dressed in his tracksuit. After grabbing his dark roast with two cubes of sugar, he slipped out onto the small terrace that overlooked the distant hills, mountains, and Sweetgum Lake. They weren't too far away, the entrance to the hiking tails and national park just up the road a half mile. It was the most beautiful view in town, in Justin's not-so-humble opinion, and he loved watching the rays of sunrise hit the mountains in the distance.

He sipped on his mug of coffee, lounging on his small wicker loveseat, as he checked his emails and business accounts on social media. The sun would be above the horizon soon; the trills and songs of birds in the nearby trees were music to his ears. It was so calming, the sleepy town surrounded in a spring-time haze as the sun started banishing shadow. Justin loved this view, and this community, setting his phone back down to simply stare at the greens and emerging yellows, whites, and pinks of the flowering peach and apple trees at the Cobbler farm on the hills beyond the Convention Hall.

The smell on the breeze, mingled with coffee, was intoxicating, and he didn't want to move from his spot as the sky turned from a hazy blue to golden yellow. However, soon he could hear the first cars on Main Street and knew that he had to start his day. He checked his watch with a smile, his routine like clockwork. Justin simply stretched, rinsed out his mug in the kitchen, and slipped on his running shoes.

He was adamant about staying in shape, content with his routine of hiking and running every morning. He didn't need anything intense like his friend Nate, the mayor's son, who was a fan of lifting weights and various forms of martial arts. No, Justin was pretty simple in comparison, locking the apartment door behind him. He was descending the main staircase from the street to his apartment side-door when he spotted the usual first face of the day. It was Ms. Everly, the local librarian, and member of the hit-and-run, power-walking squad. He called out a greeting and she smiled, waved, and kept walking, turning up the street around the block, her white hair bouncing in the slight breeze. Everyone knew not to get in the way of a member of the hit-and-run crew. The nickname was well earned.

Justin continued on, straight down Main Street, past Rochelle's Diner, and to the wide and newly re-paved sidewalk that led to the park entrance and Nature Center & Water Museum. It wasn't a long walk, reaching the park entrance within ten minutes. He spotted the old head ranger at the nearby station, Lyle, sitting on the porch and waving. After waving back with a kind smile, Justin went over to the cabin to speak to him. It had been a while since he and Lyle conversed.

In fact, Lyle was one of his few local customers, owning a watch his father had given him over fifty years ago.

"Good morning," Lyle smiled, rocking in the wooden chair. "How you been, Justin?"

"Good morning, and well," he said, leaning against the railing of the stairs. "You still keeping those young rangers in line?"

"Every day," he chuckled, his graying beard twitching. "They keep me on my toes, that's for sure."

"That's good to hear," Justin smiled, enjoying the stories Lyle had told him the last time they'd met. "Hopefully, nothing too wild…."

"Always wild around here," he winked, nodding at the rangers who were returning on horseback from the mountain trails. "They learn to ride horses and they start thinking they're cowboys…"

"I don't see any cows," Justin joked, the two sharing a laugh as the two younger rangers approached. "Well, I'll see you later, Lyle. I got an early day today but feel free to stop by whenever you like."

"I will! Enjoy, and watch out for the slides; we've had a few trails overrun with mud and rockslides since the seasons have started to turn," he warned, standing from his chair. "And there are all sorts of critters out, so be sharp."

"Thanks, Lyle; I'll make sure to be extra careful," Justin assured, waving at him. He smiled and waved at the other rangers before he rounded the ranger station and took off at a jog on his favorite trail. It went up the hills overlooking Sweetgum Lake, rounded it into the meadow, and ended back near the ranger station.

It wasn't a complicated trail, mostly small hills and only one steep incline, which was fine with him. He wasn't in his 20s anymore, so he needed to keep moving but still stay careful. It was good that he did this almost every morning, running into

Lyle on the off chance he wasn't busy with his duties and recruits. The run didn't take very long either, returning to the ranger station after a half hour. The smell of spring flowers, new leaves, and the lake was so refreshing, and Justin appreciated that Lyle left him a bottle of water on the station steps when he came back around. A little sticky note that read "For Justin" made him smile, and he took it happily, walking back to his place from there.

The sun was up now, above the horizon, and when he made it back into the main part of town, he noticed that the street clock across from the diner read seven-thirty. The sleepy town was humming by now, the early risers and schoolkids prepping for another spring day.

Justin made his way to his shop and the staircase up to his apartment with a wave to his friend and fellow business owner, Demetrius, across the street. Demetrius owned Nerd Central Comic and Video Game Store, a place that always reminded Justin of his childhood. As a kid, Justin used to eagerly wait for his dad to come home from work so they could sit together and read the latest Archie comics. They both loved how the stories were simple, wholesome, and always had a happy ending.

Justin's love for Archie comics stayed with him over the years, and when he stumbled upon Nerd Central, he found a treasure trove of vintage Archie comics and collectibles. He spent hours browsing through the store, reminiscing about his childhood, and admiring the artwork of his favorite characters. From that day on, he would often visit Demetrius and his store, and they would discuss the latest comic releases and share their favorite stories.

As Justin climbed the stairs to his apartment, he smiled at the memory of his dad's laughter as they read their favorite Archie comics together. He knew that even now, his love for these comics continued to bring joy to his life.

As a child, Justin's love for the comics wasn't just about

reading them. He would spend hours trying to recreate the characters and scenes from the comics with his paintbrushes and canvas. It was this early creative passion that led him to fall in love with painting, and he would often spend his free time experimenting with pop art styles.

However, despite his love for painting, he was hesitant to share this part of himself with anyone. He feared being judged or not taken seriously, so he kept his art hidden away in the privacy of his apartment.

Justin hopped into the shower, made another cup of coffee, dressed for work, and popped a frozen breakfast sandwich into the microwave before enjoying a few quiet moments back out on his balcony.

He usually opened at nine, but he liked getting down to the workshop early, descending the inner staircase to the back room where the rear door of the building was. The workshop was shadowy, quiet, and when he flipped the light on, it hummed overhead. He loved the smell of the cut wooden pieces as he finished his sandwich, cleaning off his hands with a clean rag before turning back to what he had been working on the day before.

Most of the shops, with the exception of Rochelle's, Roasted Beans, and the daycare, weren't open and wouldn't open until nine or ten, so he had time to relax and enjoy the intricate pieces he'd designed and started putting together for a client in Belgium. It was very rare that he did only repairs, like with Courtney's piece, his mind wandering to the very old and precious piece she brought in.

He was playing with a digital proof of a custom watch for his Belgian client when his mind wandered once again to Courtney. Today was supposed to be the day she came to help him.

As if his thoughts of her conjured her, he heard the chime of the door opening. He turned to see Courtney walking in, holding a large paper bag.

"Good morning, Justin." she walked in a little timidly. "I come bearing pastries from Roasted Beans Coffee Spot."

Justin smiled at her, feeling grateful for her thoughtfulness. "Thank you, Courtney. That's very kind of you."

"I figured we could use some fuel for the day ahead," she said with a slight grin. "And as promised, I'm here to help you out today. It's my day off from the cell phone store, and I'm happy to lend a hand."

"That's fantastic," Justin said, relieved to have some extra help. "I have a lot of watch repairs to get through today, and having an extra set of hands will definitely make things easier."

Justin led Courtney to the counter, handed her the ledger, and began explaining the basics of the watch shop to her.

"Okay, so when a customer comes in, the first thing you should do is greet them and ask if they need any assistance. If they have a watch they need repaired, we'll take it in and give them an estimate. If they're looking to buy a watch, we can show them our selection and answer any questions they have."

Courtney nodded, taking mental notes as Justin spoke. "Got it. And if they need a repair estimate, you take their information and give them a call back with the estimate?"

"Exactly," Justin said with a smile. "And if they're dropping off a watch for repair, make sure to tag it with their name and phone number, and write down any notes they have about the repair they need."

Courtney repeated the instructions back to him to make sure she had everything down. "Got it. And what should I do if a customer has a question I don't know the answer to?"

"Just let them know that you'll check with me in the back and get back to them as soon as possible," Justin replied. "And don't worry, I'll be in and out to help you as needed."

Courtney felt a little nervous but also excited to be learning something new. "Okay, I think I can do this. Thanks for explaining everything to me."

"No problem at all," Justin said with a grin. "Now, let's get to work!"

⁂

Justin disappeared into the back, leaving Courtney to handle the first customer of the day. A middle-aged man walked in, holding his watch in his hand.

"Hi, how may I help you?" Courtney asked with a warm smile.

"I need a new battery for my watch," the man replied.

"Of course, we can definitely help you with that," Courtney said. "Let me just get some information from you."

She pulled out the ledger and handed it to the man. "Would you please fill out your name, phone number, and any other information we might need?"

As the man filled out the information, Courtney took the watch from him and carefully tagged it with his name and phone number.

"Thank you, sir," Courtney said, taking the ledger back. "We'll get back to you with an estimate and let you know when your watch will be ready."

The man thanked her and left the store with a smile on his face. Courtney felt a sense of satisfaction as she watched him go.

Another customer walked into the shop, browsing the display cases. They stopped in front of one case and pointed to a particular watch. "I saw this watch the last time I was here and I couldn't stop thinking about it. I want to buy it."

Courtney smiled and walked over to the case; she recognized it as one that Justin made himself. "Great choice. It's one of our custom pieces. Let me grab the key to open the case."

She retrieved the key and unlocked the case, carefully removing the watch from its display stand. She handed it to the customer and said, "Take a closer look. It's a beauty, isn't it?"

The customer examined the watch, admiring the intricate design and details. "It's even better than I remember. How much does it cost?"

Courtney checked the price tag on the watch and said, "It's $1,500."

The customer hesitated for a moment before nodding. "I'll take it."

"Excellent," Courtney said, grabbing a sales form from behind the counter. "Just fill out this form with your information and we'll get it packaged up for you."

The customer filled out the form and handed it back to Courtney along with their credit card. "It's an investment, but I'm excited about this watch."

"I can understand why. It's gorgeous." Courtney smiled as she processed the transaction and carefully packaged up the watch. "Thank you for your purchase. You won't regret it. It's a truly unique piece."

The customer thanked her and left the shop, beaming with excitement over their new purchase.

The day went on smoothly with Courtney handling the customers like a pro. She was polite, professional, and efficient. Justin would check on her every once in a while and each time he came out, he praised her for doing such a great job.

Courtney was surprised at how much she enjoyed working in the shop. She had always loved sales, so helping customers with their watches came naturally to her. As the day progressed, the shop got busier and the phone started ringing off the hook. Courtney answered it with a smile and handled each call with ease.

Justin would come out from the back to assist with more complex questions, but for the most part, he left Courtney to handle the day-to-day tasks. She proved to be a quick learner and her customer service skills were top-notch.

As Courtney finished assisting another customer, the phone

rang as they were walking out. She rushed over and answered, "Justin Time's Clock and Watch Repair. How may I help you?"

A woman on the other end of the line asked, "Who is this?" with a snotty tone.

"This is Courtney. How may I assist you?"

"Is Justin there? That's my husband's shop."

"May I ask who's calling?"

"I just told you. I'm Maurine, his wife. I wasn't able to reach him on his cell, so I'm calling the shop."

Courtney was taken aback, not knowing that Justin was married. She stuttered, "Um, I'm sorry, I didn't know. Let me see if he's available."

She placed Maurine on hold and went to the back to inform Justin. He was visibly flustered and quickly took the phone from her as she moved aside to try and give him privacy.

"Maurine, what the hell are you doing calling my shop?" Justin's voice was stern.

"I needed to talk to you, and you weren't answering your phone," Maurine said loud enough for Courtney to hear even though Justin was holding the phone to his ear.

"That's because I don't want to talk to you. You know we're done. Stop calling me."

Courtney tried to steady her breathing, and for a moment, her mind had gone blank as she tried to process the fact that Justin was married. As she listened in on the conversation between Justin and Maurine, she felt a sense of disappointment wash over her. She had enjoyed spending time with Justin and had even started to develop feelings for him. Learning that he was married was a huge blow.

But as she continued to listen, she also felt a sense of confusion. Maurine sounded so in love with Justin, yet he was so cold and distant towards her. It was clear that there was a lot of history between them, and Courtney wondered what had gone wrong.

Courtney could hear Maurine crying on the other end of the phone as Justin hung up. Was Justin a heartbreaker? She felt bad for Maureen.

Justin looked embarrassed as he approached Courtney. "I'm sorry you had to deal with that," he said, gesturing towards the phone. "That was my ex-wife, Maurine."

Courtney's eyebrows raised in surprise. "Ex-wife? Oh, I had no idea. She was quite... dramatic," she said, choosing her words carefully.

Justin let out a humorless laugh. "Yeah, that's one way to put it. We've been divorced for a few years now, but she still calls me from time to time, trying to rekindle things."

Courtney gave him a sympathetic look and she ignored the relief she felt at his words. "That sounds tough. I'm sorry you have to deal with that."

Justin shrugged. "It's alright. I'm just sorry you got caught in the middle of it. I should have warned you that she might call."

"It's okay," Courtney reassured him. "It sounds like you handled her pretty well," she said, still feeling shaky.

Justin chuckled. "Yeah, I've had some practice over the years. But seriously, thanks for your help today. You've been a real lifesaver."

Courtney smiled. "No problem. I'm happy to help. I really enjoy sales. That's how I started working at the cellphone store."

Justin nodded in agreement. "Yeah, I know what you mean. It can be satisfying to help someone find that perfect watch or clock."

As they continued chatting, the phone rang again, causing them both to jump. This time, Justin answered it himself, speaking quietly but firmly to the person on the other end. When he hung up, he turned to Courtney with a sigh.

"That was Maurine again. I think I need to block her number or something."

Courtney nodded in understanding. "Do what you need to

do. And don't worry, I've got things covered here. You can focus on the back."

"Thanks, Courtney," Justin said, giving her a thankful smile as he disappeared into the back room once again.

As the day came to a close, Justin thanked Courtney for all of her hard work and praised her once again for doing such a great job. Courtney was grateful for the opportunity to work in the shop and excited to come back again the next time she had a day off.

As Courtney made her way home, she really wanted to know what kind of man Justin was. You could tell a lot about a man by the way he handled his past relationships. She knew it wasn't her business, but her feelings were involved, so she wanted to know how his relationship with his ex-wife ended. She didn't want to be interested in a man who played with hearts if that were the case.

CHAPTER SEVEN

*J*ustin lay in bed the next morning, staring up at the ceiling. His mind was still reeling from the phone call with his ex-wife and the awkwardness of having Courtney witness it. He wondered what she was thinking and feeling after that interaction.

As he lay there, he realized that the thought of potentially losing Courtney before anything had even begun made him uneasy. He had always been guarded, afraid of getting hurt again, but something about her made him want to take a chance.

He thought back to their interactions at the shop the day before, how she had effortlessly handled the customers and how he had felt drawn to her presence. He knew he had trust issues, but he was starting to see that he was possibly willing to open up enough to consider a romance.

Justin couldn't shake off the feeling of unease as he went about his morning routine. Did he mess up his chances with Courtney? She was smart, beautiful, and had a kind heart. He enjoyed spending time with her and he didn't want to lose that. Did she think less of him now that she knew he had been married before?

Justin was in the back room of the watch shop, preparing for the day when he heard the buzzer from the front door. He opened the unlocked door and opened it to allow Courtney to walk in with a bag from Rochelle's Old-Fashioned Diner.

"Good morning!" she said, a bright smile on her face. "I thought I'd stop by and bring us some breakfast. I hope you don't mind."

Justin was surprised but also grateful for the gesture. "Thank you, that's very kind of you," he replied.

He guided her toward the back of the shop and they sat down at the small table there, enjoying their breakfast sandwiches and coffee. As they ate, Justin felt a little awkward after what had happened with Maureen the day before.

"Listen, about yesterday…" he began, unsure of what to say.

Courtney looked up at him, her expression curious.

"I just wanted to apologize for the situation with my ex-wife. I didn't mean for you to get caught in the middle like that," Justin explained.

"It's okay," Courtney reassured him. "I'm just glad that it wasn't as bad as it sounded on the phone."

Justin was taken aback by her kindness, especially after the awkwardness of yesterday. "No, not at all. Thank you so much, Courtney," he replied, feeling his heart flutter.

Justin felt drawn to her. There was something about her that made him feel comfortable and at ease, and he found himself wanting to open up to her.

Courtney nervously fidgeted around with her napkin and looked at him nervously. "I hope I'm not being too forward, Justin, but I would be lying if I said I wasn't curious. I was wondering why you and your wife got divorced," Courtney said, avoiding his eyes.

Justin hesitated for a moment, unsure of whether he wanted to reveal his past to her. But as she looked up, after seeing the genuine look of care in her eyes, he decided to take the plunge.

"After putting you through that scene yesterday, the least I could do is tell you," he said, taking a deep breath. "She was the love of my life," he explained, unwilling to meet her eyes. "I mean, I'd been ready to give her the world, but I didn't realize what kind of woman she was. She'd been constantly looking for the next best thing, you know? The bigger, better deal."

"I'm sorry…"

"I made a good living, but not in her eyes because she came from money and no matter what I did, it wasn't enough for her. We signed a prenup because of her large inheritance," he explained, biting his lip. "I mean, money doesn't matter to me, but the prenup stipulated that it was voided if either of us were unfaithful. But, it didn't really do much to stop her from cheating."

"Oh no," Courtney whispered, pushing some of her loose curls back behind the headband she'd worn that day.

"Yeah, she had been sleeping with a partner at her father's law firm," he explained, his voice soft. "I guess it had been going on for almost six months. I mean, that's what really shook me. How could someone lie to a person they claimed to care about for six long months?"

"People can be selfish," Courtney responded, her hand finding his arm. He looked up at her now, finally, her sparkling bright eyes bringing a comfort that he couldn't describe.

"They certainly can be," he nodded, placing his hand over hers. "So, rather than draw things out in a messy divorce, she decided to offer me a lump sum to walk away quietly and not go after her inheritance," he said, rolling his eyes.

"You don't seem like the kind of guy to do that," Courtney scoffed, making him grimace. "I mean, I've only known you a week or so and you don't give me that kind of vibe."

"I didn't want it at all," he confirmed, his fingers still gently resting over hers on his forearm. "I didn't care about that. I cared that she hurt me, which she really didn't recognize, even after the divorce. No apology, no responsibility, nothing. So, I took the money she was required to give me and turned it into something positive."

"Justin Time," she smiled, looking around the workshop. "That's wonderful and I'm so happy for you. Going after your dreams and passions after something so painful takes character and dedication."

"It made me who I am now, but I couldn't be happier," he chuckled, their fingers still touching. "I mean, I love Sweetgum so much. I even love doing some of the decorations and various reenactments during Founders Day. I love the connectivity of the town and their love for history and one another."

"They can be quite nosey though," she smirked, nudging him gently with her knee. "It's a good thing, though, considering they care quite a bit about those they consider their own."

"I've noticed!" Justin smirked, staring down at their hands now. It felt so comfortable to touch her like this, to be connected in such a small but intimate way.

Courtney's expression softened as she looked at him. "But, I really am sorry, Justin. That must have been extremely hard for you," she said.

"It was, but I'm getting over it," Justin replied, appreciative of her sympathy. "And honestly, talking to you about it makes me feel better."

"I'm glad I could help," she said, smiling. "I have to get to work, but I'll stop by the next time I'm able." She said, getting up to leave.

"I look forward to it," he said, walking her to the door before getting back to work himself.

He was usually a creature of habit, of routine, but the thought of Courtney coming by to interrupt was exciting and appreciated. He couldn't be angry or annoyed about creating a new routine that involved her. It was fun to talk to her, as she was so happy and kind. He also liked the dimples in her cheeks when she smiled and the way her curls bounced when she laughed. She had such bright eyes too, her emotions showing through them effortlessly. That was something he just wasn't good at, his emotions often hiding behind a wall he preferred to keep tall and strong. His divorce had done that to him, the thought of it triggering anxiety and anger that he'd never had before.

Thinking of Maureen and what she had done to him made him realize that by closing himself off to anyone else, he was allowing her to win. He knew for a fact he wasn't getting back with his ex, and he was not the type of man who wanted to spend the rest of his life alone. But he wasn't one for casual relationships. When he gave, he gave his whole heart, and he wanted to make sure the next woman he was with gave her whole heart in return.

He wondered when Courtney would stop by again. Even if it was just lunch, or coffee, he'd be happy with it. That thought alone shocked him, that familiar anxiety rising inside his stomach and turning. He quickly shook away this thought, realizing it was almost nine now and that he should open up the shop to customers. He didn't get a lot of walk-in business in Sweetgum, most of his orders were placed from other places including overseas, but he loved the small-town setting. The community was important to Justin, more than he'd like to admit. It was his friends like Demetrius, Nate, and the other business owners in Sweetgum that helped him through some low points.

Being a part of a community was important to him, even though he mainly stuck to himself with few close friends. That didn't really matter; quality over quantity being his motto for a while now. After unlocking the front door, turning the "open" sign on, and switching on some antique lamps, he checked the clocks.

It was a few hours later, after looking closely at his Belgian order and carving some pieces, that he realized it was almost lunchtime. Although Courtney had come in for breakfast earlier that day, Justin realized he was impatiently waiting to see if she'd be back. He felt like a giddy teenager, his heart racing as the minutes ticked away. He even went to sit behind the counter, pretending to work on a piece as he waited. It was then, when he was playing with the watch, that he realized he hadn't felt this way since long before his divorce.

CHAPTER EIGHT

Courtney had finished her morning at the store, happy to leave shortly after noon. She wanted to grab something for lunch and bring it Justin. She pushed the warning out of her mind that told her she was doing too much, that she had just taken him breakfast that morning, that she would come across too strong. When she was with Justin, she didn't feel that restless feeling she had been experiencing and she wanted more of the happiness she felt when she was in his presence.

Before she went to the shop, she stopped at Sweet and Spicy Chinese Palace to get the lunch special. Since Justin's place was right next to the Chinese restaurant, it was easy to carry the small bag of goodies straight to his door. However, when Courtney grabbed the doorhandle to enter, a wave of anxiety and nervousness washed over her. It was sudden, frightening, and made her pause only a moment.

She then opened the door, swinging it inward as swayed in the doorway. She felt her curls bouncing atop her head, her appointment at the salon yesterday post-lunch with Justin much appreciated. Kim wasn't back, but her co-workers knew exactly what she wanted, and she had a good time listening to their gossip and excitement over Kim's social posts. Courtney shut the glass-pane door with a jingle, turning back to see Justin was standing at the counter already, smiling.

She was a bit shocked, as he seemed to be waiting for her. She had to shake this from her mind, waving at him happily as she approached the glass and polished wood display and countertop. It didn't mean anything, Justin was most likely being polite as she did promise she'd return. However, when he spotted the bag of goodies from Rochelle's his face lit up beautifully. Courtney was stunned by the wide warmth of his smile and the twinkle in his dark eyes as she set the bag down.

"You keep spoiling me," he chuckled, staring hungrily at the bag. "Ms. Zhang's?"

"Yup, something a bit different from this morning," Courtney smiled, admiring the dark jeans and button-up green shirt he was wearing under his simple gray sweater-vest. He also had his glasses on, Courtney unwilling to admit to herself that it made him that much more attractive.

"Come on, let's enjoy it at the table," he suggested, motioning for her to come around the counter. He grabbed up the bag gently, opening the door to the back room and workshop.

It wasn't a large room, but it was full of benches, shelves, and various small parts, equipment, and in-progress pieces. She was fascinated, her eyes going wide as she admired a tall grandfather clock along the wall. It was so intricately designed, and beautiful, each tick in time with the others that were around them. It wasn't an annoying sound like Courtney had thought, the steady hum of it comforting as Justin offered her one of his work benches around the central table in his workshop. It was half-full of carved wooden pieces, some polished, others smoothed.

He then offered her a cushion, smiling kindly as she adjusted on the stool and removed her cardigan. He took it from her kindly, his manners impeccable, as he hung it up on one of the hooks near the only other door in the room leading to the back lot and drive. He then sat down next to her at the end of the square table, happy to hand out the food.

"I wasn't sure if you'd be back today," he smiled, offering her the napkins from the bag. "I mean, this morning was a very pleasant surprise."

"I did tell you I'd be here, to help however I can," she assured, opening the lid to the noodles. "What you are doing for me, is above and beyond anything I could have expected. The least I could do is help you deal with customers and bring you food."

"Well, I'm not doing the work for free," he chuckled, a smirk forming on his face. "But I appreciate the extra effort. It's quite nice to break from my daily routine."

"I feel that," Courtney nodded, hating her recent daily routine. "I've been considering my own routine and how to shake it up."

"Well, you are always welcome here," he nodded, putting some soy sauce on the noodles.

The two ate their food in between smiles and polite comments about Mrs. Zhang's cooking and how beautiful the weather is turning. Courtney learned that it was Justin's favorite season, that he ran the Sweetgum trails every morning, and that he was working extra hard on an order from Belgium.

"I really enjoy making custom pieces," Justin explained, offering to throw away her empty container. "Tinkering, layering, and creating the little parts and details needed for an excellent watch or clock has always drawn me in."

"It shows," she complimented. "I mean, it's all so fascinating. Can I ask what brought you to Sweetgum, specifically? I mean, it is a small town, and I can't imagine you getting that much walk-in business. Is there a story behind how you got started here?"

"It's a long, complicated story," Justin admitted, his voice softer now as he returned to the table.

"Oh," Courtney nodded, not wanting to pressure him. "I didn't mean to pry...."

"No, no, it's alright," he nodded, the sadness in his eyes making her bite her lip. She wanted to know what was behind that sadness, what pain he was trying so desperately to control. She could see it in his body language, in the intensity of his dark eyes, and in the way his voice changed when he spoke. She wanted to know more, to share his pain but didn't press further.

"I actually fell in love with tinkering many years ago," he admitted, smiling at her now. "My father gave me a pocket watch when I turned thirteen, and I was instantly fascinated."

"That's how I felt about my first set of paints," Courtney said, smiling at the topic change as his eyes grew wide. "I love painting. I also love to sculpt, but not as much as painting."

"I didn't know you were an artist," he replied, leaning his elbow on the table and his cheek on his palm. "What do you paint?"

"Everything, anything. Mostly Impressionism." She looked away, the intensity of his eyes and curiosity overwhelming. "But you're an artist too. I mean, just look at all this!"

"You think?" he asked, looking around. "I mean, before I came to settle in Sweetgum, I apprenticed with a watchmaker in Nashville, making custom pieces for clients. He taught me so much and he always talked about the art of making clocks and gears."

"It's true, and I would consider myself an amateur painter, but even I can see the passion and artistry in every one of your pieces," Courtney encouraged, smiling at him. "I mean, each piece is unique and every part, every piece, is created by hand. You put your heart into it, and I think your customers can tell."

"I guess I've never thought of it that way," he chuckled, a shy smile forming as he adjusted his glasses. "But during my apprenticeship, I also learned woodworking and carpentry techniques for custom pieces."

"That's similar to sculpting," she encouraged, leaning closer. "I mean, it's just sculpting with wood and metal gears if you think about it."

"True," he laughed, nodding enthusiastically. "I mean, I wish that my clients would commission larger clock projects. Size doesn't matter when it comes to making custom pieces, but I prefer the larger clocks or mantle pieces."

"Yeah?"

"Absolutely, and I really enjoyed apprenticing with my former master," he nodded, his eyes twinkling with memory. "I actually met my ex-wife in Nashville while I was apprenticing."

"Was she also an artist?"

"Oh no, far from it," he chuckled, the sound filling Courtney with happiness. "Probably one of the reasons we didn't work out. Though, if it hadn't been for all that, I wouldn't be here in Sweetgum. Ever since I got here, I've felt nothing but happiness. I might be an outsider in some respects, but the community at large has been so inviting, accepting, and an absolute lifesaver."

"I understand that," she smiled, taking a drink from her soda bottle. "Sweetgum has been my home since the beginning and has always been there for me."

"I'm just happy to have a life that I can be proud of," he admitted, turning, and leaning against the table on his elbows. He smiled over his shoulder at her, his voice light and happy as he continued. "Owning a successful business doing what I love alongside providing a service for the community that has accepted me as one of their own. That's what makes me happy. That's what drives me."

"Do you get a lot of business here in Sweetgum, though? I mean, I'm not trying to be nosey…"

"Not a lot," he chuckled, making her blush again. "Repairs, a few gifts now and then, and of course, some people enjoy the antiques I've collected."

"So, sorry again, but… how do you make a profit?" Her business studies and tax education had kicked in, and she wasn't sure if it was too rude to ask. Usually, it would be, but he seemed genuinely happy to discuss his business.

"Most of my clients are higher-end clients, custom ordering pieces from places like New York or London or Shanghai," he said, her eyes going wide. "It's a great business and allows me to practice my passion in the place that I love. You interested in business?"

"I studied accounting and taxes at university," she replied, her voice soft. "It's steady work."

"That's smart," he nodded, grabbing up one of the small watches from the bench, turning to tinker with it as they spoke. "Do you enjoy your work?"

"I actually arrange and prepare the town taxes monthly and during tax season is when I make the bulk of my earnings for the year," she affirmed, watching him happily. "When I'm not doing that, I'm the store assistant manager at the cell store."

"A woman with many hats," he smiled, grabbing a set of tweezers to place a particularly small gear into the right slot. "I've only got a certain set of skills."

"But at least you're passionate about it," she sighed, watching him closely. "And you're really good at it. I mean, I know it's a skill you learned, but you make it look so effortless."

"You think so?" he asked, glancing over the rim of his glasses at her. "That's a great compliment, actually."

"It is most definitely a compliment," she nodded, her phone dinging in her pocket. That's when she noticed what time it was, panic rising in her. Justin noticed immediately, setting down the piece he was working on.

"Sorry," she sighed, rolling her eyes at the text message. "My regional manager is stopping in, so I have to go back to work."

"Okay," he smiled, standing from the table. "Let me at least walk you out."

"Thanks," she smiled, happy that he grabbed her cardigan

and held it open for her. She slipped into it with a nod, offering to help clean up the lunch mess, but he waved her off, following beside her as they emerged back into the shop.

"Have a good rest of your day," he smiled, opening the door for her as they approached, the bell jingling.

"I'll see you tomorrow," she said, patting his arm as she passed by. "Have a good night, Justin."

"You too, Courtney...."

COURTNEY COULD FEEL her heart pounding the whole walk back to the store, her mind completely distracted. She hadn't even realized she'd arrived back at the cell phone store until she saw her regional manager emerging from her car. Courtney's mood immediately shifted at this, the district manager waving happily. That little bit of reassurance didn't really help. She hated her job. Her store manager was supposed to be the one meeting with the regional manager today, but once again, he was nowhere to be found.

When they entered the store, the district manager looked around it critically, taking notes on a clipboard.

"Where's your manager?" she asked, looking at Courtney.

"He said he had an emergency, so he couldn't make it," she said, trying to sound as professional as possible.

The district manager rolled her eyes. "This isn't the first time he's bailed on a meeting. I swear, I don't know how he still has a job."

Courtney tried to hide her frustration. If the district manager truly felt like that, why didn't she fire him? They could've given Courtney his position and his pay. Instead, she had been running the store by herself for weeks, with little to no support from her manager. She felt undervalued and taken for granted.

The district manager continued to inspect the store, occasionally asking Courtney questions about sales and inventory. Courtney answered politely, even though she knew her store manager had all the numbers and data readily available.

As the district manager was about to leave, she turned to Courtney and said, "Thanks for your help. You're doing a great job keeping this place running."

Courtney forced a smile and nodded, but inside, she was seething. It was always the same old story—she did the work, but her manager got the credit.

As soon as the district manager left, Courtney made up her mind—she was going to start looking for another job. She deserved to be appreciated and valued for her hard work, and it was clear that wasn't going to happen at this store.

It surprised Justin when Nate mentioned joining him for his morning run on the hiking trails. He knew Nate was just as dedicated to his own fitness routine, but it had been a while since they had the chance to catch up. Justin was looking forward to having some company on the trails, and he knew that Nate would keep up with him. As they made their way to the ranger station to check in with Lyle before starting their run, Justin felt grateful for the chance to spend some quality time with his friend while also getting a good workout in.

As they ran along the trail, Justin and Nate chatted about everything from international orders for custom watches at Justin's shop to their latest workout routines. Nate had been a good friend to him since Justin had moved to Sweetgum, and he was thankful for his company. As the mayor's son, Nate made it his business to meet everyone in town, and he and Justin just clicked. Justin was also good friends with Demetrius, the local comic shop owner, and Sean, the owner of the local dance studio, and he was looking forward to meeting Chris, Nate's friend who had recently moved back to town.

"Chris has recently taken over as the new librarian. He's a cool dude; you'll like him," Nate said as they slowed down to catch their breath.

"I'm sure I will," Justin replied. "It'll be nice to have a guys' night with all of us."

"I was thinking we could do some poker or board games," Nate suggested. "What do you think?"

"Sounds like a plan," Justin agreed. "Demetrius said we could meet up at his shop since he already has all the games and stuff there. It's been a while since I've played some good old-fashioned board games."

Nate laughed. "I know what you mean. I'm looking forward to hanging out with the guys."

Justin nodded in agreement. "Definitely. I'm looking forward to it, too."

As they continued jogging along the trail, Nate suddenly turned to Justin and sighed heavily. "You know, man, India and I decided to break up," he said, looking a little down.

Justin frowned in sympathy. "I'm sorry to hear that, man. Is everything okay?"

Nate nodded. "Yeah, we're both okay with it. It was just one of those things, you know? We realized we were better off as friends. We weren't really compatible in the long run, and we were just forcing it. It's better this way."

Justin nodded understandingly. "I hear you. It's tough, but sometimes it's better to end things before they get worse. I'm here for you if you need anything."

Nate smiled gratefully. "Thanks, man. I appreciate it. It's just weird being single again. I feel like I don't know what to do with myself."

Justin chuckled. "Well, we can always move up the date for that guys' night you were talking about. Maybe it'll cheer you up."

Nate brightened up at the idea. "Yeah, let me get with

Demetrius and see what night would be best." As they jogged around a bend, Nate asked, "So, Justin, have you heard from Maureen lately?"

Justin shook his head, "No, I blocked her from calling me. I'm done with that chapter of my life."

Nate looked surprised, "Wow, what made you finally decide to block her?"

"I met someone," Justin replied with a small smile.

Nate raised his eyebrows, "Oh really? I'm really curious about anyone who could make you break your 'no women rule.' Who is she?"

"Her name is Courtney," Justin said, "She's been helping me out at the watch shop."

Nate nodded, "Ah, I think I remember you mentioning her before. Wait. Courtney… Courtney…" His face was squinched up in concentration. "Yeah, I know her. She's friends with India's sister Nevaeh. She's also friends with Chris' fiancé, Brandi. So, things are going well?"

"Boy, everyone really does know everyone around here," Justin laughed. "Yeah, they are. I don't know where it's going, but I'm interested in finding out. I haven't said anything to her about my feelings, though. I'm just trying to feel things out and see where it leads. I think she might be interested, too."

Nate grinned, "That's great to hear, man. You deserve some happiness after everything you've been through."

Justin shrugged, "Yeah, I guess I do. But I'm also trying not to get too ahead of myself. I'm not going to act like I'm fixed from what Maureen did to me, but I feel like I'm healing."

Nate nodded, "I understand that, and I get it. But just enjoy it. Life's too short not to take chances."

As they continued their run, Justin felt thankful for his friend's support and encouragement. As they reached the end of the trail, Nate slowed down and stretched out his arms. "Thanks for letting me join you on this run, man. I needed that."

Justin nodded. "Anytime, bro. We should do it again soon."

Nate smiled. "Definitely. Oh, and sorry about dumping my relationship drama on you."

Justin waved it off. "It's all good, man. That's what friends are for, right?"

Nate nodded. "Yeah, you're right. Thanks for listening."

They gave each other a quick bro hug before Nate jogged off down the street.

Justin watched him go before turning and heading back toward the shop. He had a full day of watchmaking ahead of him, but it was Courtney's day off from the cell phone store, so he was looking forward to working with her. As he climbed the stairs to his apartment above the shop, he felt excited about the day ahead.

CHAPTER TEN

ourtney walked into the watch shop where Justin was already hard at work. He greeted her with a smile and asked, "I've been curious. You've mentioned that you've been painting more lately. How's it going?"

Courtney grinned, "It's been great. I actually finished an abstract piece last night called Breaking the Chains."

"Sounds powerful," Justin said, genuinely interested. "What's the inspiration behind it?"

"Well," Courtney explained, "the chains represent the weight of societal expectations and stereotypes. The woman breaking free from them symbolizes her struggle to break free and find her own path."

"That's deep; I'd love to see it," Justin said, nodding in appreciation. "Hey, would you like to display the piece here in the shop? It sounds like it would be a great addition to our decor."

Her face was slack with shock at the offer, "Are you serious? You haven't even seen it! It could be a dumpster fire for all you know!"

"I feel like I'm coming to know you, and I know that you're a hard worker and take pride in everything that you do. So, if you're excited about this painting, I know it's good. Bring it by and we can display it."

Courtney's face lit up, "I would love that! Thank you so much."

"Of course! It's a win-win for me. It will give this place more character, and I'll also get to see your work." Justin smiled at Courtney's excitement and enthusiasm for her art. "I'm serious. We could hang it up right over there," he pointed to an empty spot on the wall. "It would fit in perfectly with the aesthetic of the shop."

Courtney nodded in agreement. "I think it would look great there."

"Awesome," Justin said, clapping his hands together. "I'll make sure to get it hung up when you bring it in."

"Thanks for giving me the opportunity to display it," Courtney said, still beaming with joy.

Justin gave her a nod before heading to the back to start working. Courtney couldn't wait to see her painting up on the wall and share it with others.

She was still lost in her excitement when the phone rang, making her jump. She cleared her throat, and after the third ring, she answered.

"Hello, Justin Time's Clock and Watch Repair," she said, her voice light and bubbly. "This is Courtney; what can I help you with today?"

"Hello dear, my name's Caroline," an older-sounding woman responded, her accent unfamiliar. "I was hoping I could talk to Justin about a custom piece I'd like ordered for my anniversary in six weeks."

"That's not a problem; I will be happy to help you with anything you might need," Courtney smiled, grabbing the nearest pen and pad of paper. "Justin is currently occupied, but I would be happy to work with you and ensure he has all the details. Would this be alright, Caroline?"

"Oh yes, that's fine," she replied, her voice at ease. "I am looking to have my locket incorporated into an antique pocket watch that's been part of my husband's family for three generations."

"That sounds like a lovely and unique idea!" Courtney replied, writing down the details. "And you need this shipped out to you, yes?"

"Yes, dear," she replied, her voice full of happiness. "It will probably take a week to ship to me via courier service, so I would need this done as soon as possible."

"Understandable; it's an important piece, and we have to make sure it gets there in time," Courtney assured, writing that down. "Are you needing just a quote, or can I convince you to commit to a commission today?"

"I was asking around, and a friend referred me to Justin," she explained, Courtney happy to listen. "I was looking to just get a quote for now...."

"I can understand that, but let me ask you something, Caroline," Courtney spoke as Justin came out of the backroom to get something and noticed her on the phone. "You need this order as soon as possible, right?"

"I do..."

"And you trust your friend who recommended Justin?"

"I do."

"And are you willing to take more time to shop around and risk not having the piece in time?"

Justin stepped up to the counter now, worry written on his face, but Courtney just smiled, raising her hand to calm him. He still watched her, biting his lip, as she listened to Caroline on the other end of the line.

"You're right; I guess I'm not willing to risk it," she finally responded, a chuckle in her voice. "But can it be done?"

"Incorporating a locket into a pocket watch?" Courtney

asked, looking directly at Justin for an answer. "What kind of pocket watch is it, again?"

"It's a silver-plated Zenith from 1924," she explained, Courtney repeating the information for Justin to hear. When he nodded his approval, Courtney smirked, turning back to the conversation with Caroline.

"He can absolutely handle that, Caroline," she affirmed. "So, how about we do this… we'll arrange for the locket to be couriered to the shop as part of the deposit price, and we can guarantee return delivery within five weeks."

Justin smiled, listening to her as he stepped closer to read her notes. She felt the heat of his closeness, causing goosebumps to rise on her arms. Courtney cleared her throat.

"That's reasonable, but what's the damage?" Caroline asked, Justin hearing her. He wrote down a number on the pad of paper, making Courtney smile as she responded.

"It'll be $2,500 with a $250 deposit that covers the courier service," Courtney explained, reading Justin's neat handwriting.

"Very reasonable," the woman said, and Courtney gave Justin a thumbs-up. "I'll be happy to wire the deposit over for the courier service, and you can arrange the pickup with them."

"That's perfectly fine, Caroline. Just let me make sure I've got your address and information so we can be sure everything is arranged smoothly," Courtney smiled. "An anniversary gift is an important delivery, and we want to be sure you get it in time."

"Thank you so much, dear; you've been so helpful," the older woman responded, her voice full of excitement. "You're a very talented saleswoman."

"Thank you so much, Caroline," Courtney nodded, smiling up at Justin, who watched her with disbelief and admiration. "So, that address…."

After finishing the conversation and confirming the address, she hung up with goodbyes and encouraging words. Justin was standing by with a wide smile on his face when she finally hung up.

"That was amazing," he admitted, leaning against the counter. "I'm impressed. You need a job?" The chuckle in his voice signaled he was joking.

"Is that a real offer, or are you teasing me?" she asked, winking at him slyly.

"Would you consider a legitimate offer?" he asked, his eyes going wide.

"I would," she responded, nodding her head. "I'd much rather spend my days here, in this shop, than in that horrible cell store. I'd still do my tax stuff because it is steady work, but at least here, I have passion for what I'm doing."

"Really?" he asked, looking surprised and beyond happy, his dark eyes almost glowing as he watched her.

"Yes, really," she confirmed, nudging him. "Make me an offer..."

"Monday to Friday, open to close, except during tax season," he replied, nudging her back. "There's an hourly wage, but your main salary would be commission based, but I have steady work. What do you say to twenty percent of the commissions, starting with the one you just got?"

"I say deal," she affirmed, happy over such a generous offer. "I'll call my regional manager and give her my two-week notice."

She stood from the stool behind the counter now, smirking at him as she pulled her phone out. She could see Justin was still in disbelief, so she squeezed his arm gently as she made the call. The district manager, whom she had known for years, seemed shocked and tried to offer her better pay and benefits, but she wasn't having it. It was too little, too late. Courtney had finally found a job she could be passionate about. It was what she'd wanted, and the fact that she would be spending time with Justin every day was like a cherry on top.

ON HER WAY TO work the following day, Courtney stopped by Justin's shop, excited to show him her painting. Her heart skipped a beat as she saw Justin's handsome face. "Hey," she greeted him, trying to keep her cool. "I brought the painting."

Justin smiled warmly at her. "Great, let's take a look," he said, leading her to the wall where he had cleared a space for her artwork.

As he unwrapped the painting, Courtney watched his every move, admiring the way his hands moved with care and precision. When he finally turned to her, she could see the awe in his eyes.

"This is amazing," he said, his voice full of genuine admiration. "You're a great artist, Courtney. I mean, really great."

Her face heated at his words, feeling a warmth spread throughout her body. "Thank you, Justin. I'm so glad you like it."

He nodded, studying the painting more closely. "You know, there's something really special about this piece. The woman breaking the chains, it's so powerful. It's like she's fighting for her freedom, and she's not going to stop until she gets it."

Courtney smiled at his words, feeling a connection with him that went beyond the painting. "That's exactly what I was going for," she said. "It's about breaking free from the expectations and stereotypes that have been holding me back."

Justin's eyes met hers, and she could feel the electricity between them. "You're much more than you give yourself credit for, Courtney. Your work should be displayed in a gallery."

Courtney shrugged, trying to downplay her talent. "I don't know about that. I just paint because I love it."

Justin shook his head, his eyes locked on hers. "People would pay a lot of money for this. As a matter of fact, I'm going to be your first customer. I'm giving you $1,000 for the painting." He reached for his checkbook and wrote out a check for $1,000, handing it to Courtney as she stood there in shock.

"I can't accept this," Courtney said, pushing the check back towards Justin. "I didn't create this painting for money. It's just something that came from my heart."

"I understand that," Justin said, taking the check back and holding it out to her again. "But think of it this way—this is just the beginning of your career as an artist. You deserve to be compensated for your work, especially something as beautiful as this. And who knows, maybe this will give you the motivation to keep creating."

Courtney thought about it for a moment, considering his words. Justin was right. She had never thought about making money from her art. But as she looked at the painting and then back at Justin's eager face, she realized that he truly believed in her.

"Okay, I'll take it," Courtney said, finally giving in and accepting the check. "Thank you, Justin. You have no idea what this means to me."

"I think I do," Justin said, smiling warmly. "I can't wait to see what you create next."

She could feel her heart racing with excitement and a hint of something more. "I don't know what to say, Justin. But, thank you again."

He smiled at her, his gaze lingering for a moment longer than necessary. "You're welcome, Courtney. I believe in you."

As she left the shop, Courtney felt a flutter of excitement in her chest. She knew that her attraction to Justin was growing stronger every day, and she couldn't wait to see where it would lead them.

CHAPTER ELEVEN

It was two weeks later, the beautiful late April day mirroring Courtney's excited mood. She was finally starting her first day at Justin Time's and couldn't be happier. Her friends were so excited for her, and Joanne insisted that she and Justin come in for coffee at a discount for lunch to celebrate her new job. Of course, Courtney insisted they pay full price; her friend was just being overly generous about this. Joanne, Neveah, and Brandi had already held a girl's night in her honor to celebrate the night before.

"Good morning," Justin smiled, letting her in through the back door of the workshop twenty minutes before they opened. She had hoped she didn't overdress for the occasion. She chose a stylish yet professional look, wearing a tailored navy blue blazer over a white silk blouse with a tasteful collar. Her black pencil skirt hugged her curves in all the right places, and she paired it with a pair of sleek black pumps. She added a touch of personality with a silver pendant necklace and a pair of dangling earrings that sparkled in the light.

"Good morning," she responded, her matching silver headband highlighting the curls in her hair. "I was so nervous, so I hope I'm not too dressy...."

"Nonsense," he nodded, motioning to his own outfit of stylish black slacks, a white button-down shirt, and a black vest with a gray pocket square. "It looks like we have the same taste in color and clothes."

"Let me adjust this," she smiled, fixing the tucked corner of the square in his jacket with a smile. "There, perfect."

"Let me show you where you'll be working," he said, taking her out of the workshop to the storefront, but seeing her painting on the wall caught her off guard. It startled her each time she saw it. Her heart swelled with pride and joy, seeing her artwork displayed in the place she would be working. She still couldn't believe it.

Justin led her to another door behind the counter that Courtney had always assumed was a storage closet, but her jaw dropped when he opened it.

"Do you like it?" he asked, showing off the small eight-by-eight room.

It was painted white, with small wooden panels around the ceiling and baseboard. There was a nice wooden desk inside, where a laptop, phone, printer-fax machine, and lamp sat. There were also shelves on the wall, the single window framed with a clean pale curtain. The shelves held storage boxes, folders, and various bookkeeping materials that she would need. She was blown away that this had been here the whole time, but it smelled like It was newly painted.

"It's wonderful," she breathed, stepping through to sit behind the desk in the comfortable office chair. "I had no idea this was here."

"Oh, it used to just be a storage closet for random pieces and extras," he chuckled, motioning around. "But I took some time earlier this week to clear it, paint it, and ensure you had your own space. There's even a phone line in here for you."

"It's wonderful, Justin!" she smiled, spinning in the chair. "Thank you so much."

"It's not a problem," he responded, shaking his head. "You need a space to work on clerical tasks, sales, and tax stuff, so I figured I'd finally get to cleaning this place out."

"That was really considerate," she affirmed, looking directly up at him. "Seriously, thank you for the effort and care."

"Do you need anything else?" he asked, eager to help. "There are pens, pencils, sticky notes, notebooks, account books, and folders in the desk."

"You've thought of everything," she giggled, standing from her chair. "This is wonderful, truly."

"If you need anything, ask," he insisted, turning from the small room. "I'm going to flip the sign and unlock the door."

"I'll handle the customers and calls, so don't worry," she affirmed, making sure she could see the front door of the shop as she sat back down in her chair.

JUSTIN WAVED at her as he disappeared back into the workshop, focusing on the commission she had secured him from Caroline two weeks ago. He was almost done with it already; surprisingly, the locket and pocket watch were compatible. He just needed to make a few alterations, but he felt busy between this order, the one from Belgium, two from Japan, and one from New York. He hadn't looked at Courtney's piece in over a week and felt bad about that, but he was determined to get back to it as soon as he finished his order.

Four hours later, while working on a few small pieces for the locket-watch, he realized he was hungry. His stomach was rumbling, and the day had been quiet, a perfect excuse for early lunch. He set aside his work, stood from his stool, and strode to the front door to lock it. He'd go next door to order some egg rolls and dumplings, something he was looking forward to. However, when he turned around from locking the door, Courtney was standing at the counter, smiling widely. This made him jump, a colorful curse escaping his lips. She chuckled at this, waving sheepishly.

"Forgot about me already, huh?" she asked, placing her hands on her hips.

"I did," he admitted, averting his gaze in embarrassment. "I'm not used to having an employee…."

"I get that," she smirked, peering around him at the door. "You don't have to lock it. You going to get lunch?"

"I am," he nodded, glancing at the takeout menu behind the counter. "Oh! How rude of me. Do you want some?"

"I do," she affirmed, grabbing the menu and handing it to him. "I'll have the egg drop soup and some teriyaki chicken."

"I'll pay," he insisted, feeling sheepish. "Since I was rude and forgot about you."

"You were hard at work," she smiled, nodding at her office. "And that's my job, isn't it? Giving you time and space to tinker and work?"

"Well, I guess so," he chuckled, still feeling silly. "But you're a great saleswoman, so I appreciate you coming to work for me."

"You go get some lunch, and I'll hold down the fort," she laughed, squeezing his shoulder gently. She then strode around him, her hips swaying as she went to unlock the door again and turn the sign back. "Can you grab me a lemon iced tea, too?"

"Absolutely," he responded, chiding himself for staring at her curves before returning to his workshop to make the call next door. He couldn't believe he had forgotten about her, shaking his embarrassment as he dialed Mrs. Zhang.

"Hello, Sweet and Spicy Chinese Palace," Mrs. Zhang answered, her voice ringing. "How can I help you?"

"Hi, Mrs. Zhang, it's Justin," he smiled, hearing her recognition over the line.

"Ah, the usual?" she asked, making him smirk.

"Yes, dumplings and two egg rolls," he affirmed. "But also, an order of egg drop soup and teriyaki chicken."

"Oh, you're hungry today!" she trilled, making him chuckle. "Busy day?"

"Oh, a productive day for sure," he admitted, smiling over at Courtney, who sat behind the counter contently. "The extra is for Courtney."

"She's been there an awful lot lately," the older woman implied, her voice full of interest and curiosity. "What's going on there?"

"She's working for me, actually, as a saleswoman, clerk, and tax expert," he explained, Courtney beaming at his new job description. "Started today."

"Oh! I had heard something about this at book club," she admitted, the noise of pots and pans in the background. "Don't worry; I'll have your order in ten minutes."

"Thanks, Mrs. Zhang," Justin smiled, knowing she'd be gossiping about this with Rochelle and the others before the day ended.

After he hung up, he told Courtney how long it would take and offered to go down the block to the store for some drinks. He didn't recognize the feeling in his chest at first, arriving at the convenience store up the block with a smile. He hadn't realized he was smiling and paused to remind himself that nothing was actually happening.

She was just his new employee, a nice woman who needed his help with her antique watch. She was stunning, funny, kind, confident, and fun, but that didn't mean anything. He had to remind himself of this as he walked back from the store to the restaurant. When he got there, Mrs. Zhang was smiling at him, his order ready for pickup.

"How's it going over there?" she asked, nodding toward his shop. "You treating her good? She's great, isn't she?"

"You read my mind," he admitted, watching her eyes grow wide. He ducked his head slightly before paying for the food and waving goodbye. He could hear her calling after him with encouragement, but all he could keep thinking was that he didn't know where this was going or what to think. His doubts and reluctance were still holding him back, and he had no idea how to approach it.

CHAPTER TWELVE

Founders day was a few days away now, the May 16th celebration creating the usual excitement throughout the small town of Sweetgum. The main street was decorated with fresh flower baskets, ribbons, flags, and the traditional "Founder's Day" banner strung across the gazebo and stage in the down square. Each shop had flags, banners, flower baskets, and historically reproduced art or photographs of their particular building, if it existed, during the founding.

It was a huge deal here, the downtown area vibrant with color and historical photos and paintings of "Old Sweetgum" in business windows and banners. The town was buzzing leading up to the day and it made Courtney really happy to see. On her way to work at the watch shop, the locals repeatedly stopped her to talk to her. She loved that, talking to Ms. Everly the librarian, Lyle, the park ranger, and seeing Brandi and Chris at Joanne's café before finally escaping to get to work.

She didn't want to be late, crossing the street and briskly walking with the carrier of coffee cups. She was about to enter the shop when Mrs. Zhang spotted her. She stepped right in front of Courtney, blocking her path. Courtney found herself becoming slightly impatient with the kind older woman.

"How are you this morning, dear?" she asked, her usual blue-jean overalls and a crisp, clean button-up covered in a jean jacket. Courtney had always admired Mrs. Zhang for her unique style; today was no different.

"Good, headed into work here," she nodded, grimacing as she spotted Justin watching her from inside with a smirk.

"Ah, yes, Justin said you were working here," she smiled, a twinkle in her curious brown eyes. "If I'd have known you wanted a new job, I'd have offered!"

"Oh, I'm actually really enjoying this job," Courtney smiled, pushing a stray hair behind her ear as she balanced the cardboard tray of coffee.

"I can imagine," Mrs. Zhang gave an exaggerated wink, making Courtney shift uncomfortably on her feet.

"You're incorrigible!" Courtney gasped dramatically, clutching her chest, causing Mrs. Zhang to burst out in laughter.

"Nonsense, I'm supportive, deary," she winked again, nudging her gently. "You need anything, let me know. Maybe you can come to my restaurant for your first date. Nothing gets the blood flowing like my spicy kung pao."

"I'm going to tattle on you Mrs. Z," Courtney laughed, straightening her navy-blue dress with her free hand. "The whole book club is going to think you're trying to play matchmaker again."

"Oh no, this one is all on you," she smirked, turning to the window of Justin Time's. She waved enthusiastically at Justin, who emerged from behind the counter, before pointing to Courtney and giving a thumbs up.

Courtney could feel the flush on her face as Mrs. Zhang kissed her cheek and turned toward her restaurant. Courtney watched her disappear inside the restaurant alleyway before turning to Justin. He was standing in the doorway with a half-smile, leaning against the frame with crossed arms. Courtney fanned herself at the picture he presented. The man was gorgeous. However, she knew she had to rein herself in as she walked over to him, offering him the cardboard holder of coffee.

"Interesting morning?" he asked, checking his watch. "You were almost late. I was getting worried…."

"Oh, no, I've been running into people all morning," Courtney said, smiling at him as he stepped aside for her to enter.

"I love Founder's Day preparations," he smiled, shutting the shop door with a jingle. "And thanks for the coffee. You've been spoiling me with this good stuff. I might never have to brew my own again."

"Joanne knows what she's doing," Courtney insisted, smiling at him over her shoulder as she rounded the counter. "How are the orders going? You've shipped the one to Belgium?"

"Courier came and picked it up last night after we closed," he nodded. "And I'm finishing the proof and design for my Japanese client today."

"Perfect," Courtney nodded, opening her office door. "I've had emails from a social-media influencer in Atlanta who is interested in a custom piece, by the way. I explained you would have availability in two weeks to discuss the design and details. Is that good for you?"

She set her purse on the desk, sliding into her office chair as Justin offered her the other coffee. He leaned in the doorway now, watching her as she switched on the laptop and office light.

"I'm fine with that," he replied finally, his eyes still on her. "I should be finished with that anniversary gift for Caroline by then."

"Awesome, I'll make sure to update her," she winked, sipping from her cup. "I'm so excited for Founder's Day this year. It's the 150th year, you know?"

"I do," he chuckled. "I'm also really excited about it. I've found some things here in the store that I wanted to use for the Historical Society's displays."

"Really?" Courtney asked, wanting to know what they were.

"Yeah, come here," he waved, encouraging her to follow him. "I've got three pieces. One is an old oil lamp that used to sit right outside here, on that cast-iron pole. It dates from 120 or so years ago and was made in Savannah."

"Oh! The one on the shelf," Courtney smiled, staring up at the familiar bronze and iron piece that sat up on the highest shelf above the counter. "I've admired this piece more than once."

"And I also have a collector's item," he said, pointing into the display case. "A pocket watch designed in Atlanta and purchased for the town's first official mayor over 100 years ago."

"That's not a collector's item; that's a piece of history," she said, looking at the small silver watch and chain on the pillowed stand inside. "It's a beautiful piece. I've noticed it more than once now but didn't dare take it out of the case."

"Here," he insisted, unlocking the case with the small keychain attached to the cash register. "Feel how light it is. Made of silver and etched with a unique engraving."

"It's so beautiful," she sighed, letting him place it in her hand gently. "It's so lightweight…"

"It's intricately made with tempered steel, some of the first tempered steel gears used in Georgia," he nodded, flipping it in her hand. "And look at the engraving."

"To the man who overcame…" she read. "It's so beautiful and perfect for Founder's Day. Did you display them last year?"

"I did, but there is a new addition," he smiled. "An amazing piece I actually got out of a storage container here in town."

"Really?" she asked, eyes wide as she put the watch back

gently. She locked the case as Justin disappeared back into his workshop. He reappeared a short time later, his arms around something larger than she was expecting.

"It's the very first bell installed at the firehouse back in 1907," he smirked, uncovering the bronze bell.

It was glimmering with flecks of copper, green, and bronze, but across the front of it was the clear words: *Sweetgum F.D.* She couldn't believe it, reaching out to touch the rough surface with her fingertips. It was beautiful, the waves of color and worn metal shimmering beneath the greenish blue of the weathering. She ran her fingers over the surface a few times before smiling at Justin, who seemed equally fascinated by this piece of history.

"I'm going to attempt to polish it and hang it at our display in the town square," he nodded, admiring the bell. "It's a perfect piece to add to the many others."

"How about I write some little plaques?" she suggested, still admiring the bell in his hands as they slowly gravitated closer to one another. "I could type something up about the history of each piece, purchase some card stock, and we can display the history alongside the collection."

"Brilliant," he breathed, their eyes meeting for the longest moment. Courtney could feel her cheeks heating, his smile widening as they stared. His dark but trimmed beard was irresistibly touchable, having to stop herself from reaching out to cradle his face in her hand. She'd wanted to touch him for a while now but didn't want to cross a line with him. After all, he was technically her boss.

Justin took a deep breath and met Courtney's eyes, his face contorting with emotion. The air between them felt thick with tension, and Courtney's heart began to pound in her chest. Was he finally going to make a move?

"There's... something I need to tell you," Justin finally spoke, his voice heavy with the weight of what he was about to say. He no longer looked happy, and Courtney wondered what in the world it could be when they were just smiling.

Courtney felt her stomach drop as she braced herself for the worst. She watched as Justin put away his tools, the silence between them only adding to her growing anxiety.

As Justin motioned for her to sit beside him, Courtney's hands began to shake. She straightened her dress and tried to steady her breathing, but the anticipation was almost unbearable. Did she do something wrong? Did he notice her attraction? Was she about to fire her? All these thoughts ran through her mind.

"What is it?" she finally asked, her voice barely above a whisper.

"I… don't think your family watch is repairable," Justin said, his voice barely audible. "I've been trying, but the parts are so difficult to find, and I just don't think there's anything more I can do."

For a moment, Courtney sat there in stunned silence. This wasn't what she was expecting him to say, although she knew it was a possibility. She had hoped against hope that Justin would be able to fix the watch, but now it seemed all her efforts had been for nothing. Her heart felt heavy with disappointment and despair, knowing that the pocket watch had stopped working while in her care.

She managed a weak smile, trying to keep her composure. "I understand," she said softly. "Thank you for being honest with me."

The words felt hollow in her mouth, and she knew that she was going to have to find a way to come to terms with this loss. But for now, she simply sat there, feeling the weight of Justin's words sinking in.

"I'd fix it if I could," Justin whispered, sitting on the stool next to her and grabbing her hands in comfort.

"I know you would," she admitted, looking at his hands on

hers in her lap. "I knew there was a good chance it wouldn't be fixed, but it still hurts."

"I'm so sorry, Courtney," he said softly, squeezing her hands gently. "I won't give up, but at this point, I am worried the piece is beyond repair."

"I appreciate that more than you could possibly know," she said as she met his beautiful dark eyes. "But from now on, it will simply be an heirloom, something to display like all the beautiful things here. Perhaps that is the best idea? Allowing you to display it in the shop…."

"You should keep it; put your own display up in your home," he said, squeezing her hands again. His palm was so large and warm, and she didn't want him to let go.

"I think it would hurt more to see it at home," she reasoned, her voice soft. "I mean, at home, there is only me to admire it. But here, anyone can admire it."

"Well, think of it this way," he encouraged, leaning closer. "It just means that the moment it stopped is immortalized."

"You mean the moment I was crossing the street?" she said skeptically, meeting his eyes again.

"No, the moment that brought you into this shop," he chuckled, his breath hot on her face. "It immortalizes the moment for you and your decision to break your chains. Look at where this watch has brought you."

"Thank you," she sighed, biting her lip shyly.

She couldn't stop her mind from rushing through her emotions, the idea of immortalizing the moment she met him making her heart flutter. She knew it would be an absolutely adorable way for them to start a relationship, to symbolize their moment, but she was definitely getting ahead of herself. He could have been being friendly, and she still didn't want to cross that professional line.

"We better get to work," she finally sighed, squeezing his hands in return. "The Japanese design, yes?"

"R-right!" he croaked; his smile was wide as he slowly let go of her hands. "My Japanese buyer is one of my best customers."

"Go, go, I'll join you later," she smiled, turning back to her office.

Courtney sat at her desk, her face still warm, as she tried to calm herself down. She was happy to have gotten an iced coffee this time, the cool sweetness of it helping her to calm her nerves and focus.

As she sat there regaining her composure, the bell over the door jingled, and she went out to greet the customer.

There stood an impeccably dressed woman with dark flawless skin, perfectly styled hair and nails, and an air of wealth and privilege. She looked like she could buy the entire store without batting an eye and was definitely not a resident of Sweetgum.

"Welcome to Justin Time's. How may I help you?" Courtney asked with a smile.

"I need to speak to my husband immediately," the woman demanded, looking around the shop with disdain.

"Your husband?" Courtney repeated, confused, the smile slipping off her face. "I'm sorry, but I think you have the wrong location."

"I'm Maureen, Justin's wife," the woman said proudly, standing tall and confident.

Courtney's eyes widened in shock as she realized who Maureen was. She tried to keep her cool and not show her emotions, but her heart was pounding in her chest. She looked at the woman with a mix of confusion and pity.

"I'm sorry, but Justin is busy at the moment. Can I help you with anything?" Courtney replied, trying to keep her voice steady, hoping to diffuse the situation.

"I need to speak to him right now!" Maureen shouted, stomping her foot, her voice echoing in the small shop. "And who are you, anyway? His new girlfriend?"

"I'm just a friend and business associate of Justin's," Courtney said, taking a step back from the woman's aggressive stance. "Please, let's try to keep this professional."

But Maureen wasn't interested in being professional. "I need to speak with him right now, and I won't take no for an answer," Maureen retorted, her voice raising a notch. Courtney could see the anger and hurt in her eyes, and it made her feel uncomfortable.

At that moment, Justin emerged from the back of the shop, his face twisted in anger as he saw Maureen.

"What the hell are you doing here, Maureen?" he growled, his fists clenched.

"I came to talk to you, Justin," Maureen said, her voice trembling with emotion. "I miss you so much. I'm sorry I cheated on you. I was young and stupid. Please forgive me."

Justin shook his head, his anger not subsiding. "We're over, Maureen. You need to leave. This is next-level stalker stuff that you're doing right now. You've graduated from calling to showing up at my place of business. If you don't leave, I'm going to call the police and file a restraining order."

Maureen's eyes darted to Courtney, and she sneered, flicking her hand toward Courtney dismissively. "Is it because of her? You've never blocked my calls before; now, all of a sudden, I'm blocked. I know you can't possibly want her over me. Look at her and look at me. She has nothing on me."

Justin surprised Courtney by stepping in front of her and defending her. "Don't you dare talk about her like that. Courtney is an amazing woman, and she's done nothing wrong. You don't even come close to comparing with her."

This only seemed to enrage Maureen even more. She lunged around the counter towards Courtney, her hand raised as if to strike her. But Justin grabbed her and pushed her out of the shop; his face contorted in anger.

"I'm calling the police, and if you're here when they get here, I'm pressing charges." He warned, locking the door behind her.

Courtney stood there in shock, her heart racing as she realized how dangerous the situation had become. She looked at Justin with gratitude, knowing that he had just defended her against his ex-wife.

Maureen ran to her car and sped off, leaving Courtney and Justin standing there in the aftermath of the encounter. Courtney was shaken but grateful for Justin's protection. "Thank you," she whispered.

"I'm sorry you had to go through that," he said, his eyes filled with concern. "Are you okay?"

Courtney nodded, still in shock from what had just happened. "Yeah, I'm okay. Thanks for being here."

"Of course," Justin said, placing a hand on her shoulder. "I'm going to call the police and file a report. She's been harassing me for months now, and I can't let her get away with this."

Courtney watched as Justin walked over to the phone and called the police. She could hear his voice shaking slightly as he explained the situation to the operator. He gave them Maureen's name and description, as well as the make and model of her car.

When he hung up the phone, he turned back to Courtney. "They said they'll send officers over to take a statement," he said, running a hand through his hair. "I just can't believe she would do something like this."

Courtney nodded, still trying to process everything that had happened. "Do you think she'll come back?" she asked, feeling a bit uneasy.

"I don't know," Justin said, looking at her with concern. "But if she does, we'll be ready for her." He walked over to the door and locked it, turning to face Courtney with a determined expression. "I won't let her hurt you or anyone else again."

CHAPTER THIRTEEN

An hour later, Justin stood in the front of the shop with Courtney next to him, both still shaken up from the altercation with Maureen. The chime jingled above the door as it opened and two officers from the Sweetgum Police Department stepped in, introducing themselves as Officers Johnson and Smith.

"Mr. Clark, we received a call from your shop about a disturbance. Can you tell us what happened?" Officer Johnson asked, his pen and notepad ready.

Justin took a deep breath and recounted the events from earlier, explaining that Maureen was his ex-wife and had been trying to contact him for months. He told them about her showing up at the shop and demanding to speak with him and how she tried to attack Courtney when he refused to see her.

Officer Smith furrowed his brow. "Has she been violent before?"

"No, not physically," Justin replied, "but she's been harassing me with calls and messages. I've told her repeatedly that it's over and to leave me alone, but she won't listen."

Officer Johnson nodded, taking notes. "We'll need you to

come down to the station and file a report. We can also issue a restraining order if you'd like."

"I'd appreciate that," Justin said, feeling relieved that the police were taking this seriously.

Courtney spoke up, "Officers, I was a witness to what happened. If you need, I can give a statement, too."

Officer Smith turned to her, "Absolutely, we'll need your account of the incident as well."

As they were finishing up, the door opened again, and two more officers walked in, flashing their badges showing they were from Atlanta.

"Excuse us, Officers," the first officer said. "We were instructed to come over and handle this case."

Officer Johnson and Smith looked at each other, confused.

"On whose authority? This is our jurisdiction." Officer Smith stated.

"These papers should explain everything," the second officer said, handing them a document.

As they read over the paperwork, Officer Johnson let out a sigh, "I see. We'll step aside and let you handle this." The Sweetgum officers looked sullen as they handed over the case to the Atlanta officers and left the shop.

One of the Atlanta officers, a tall and imposing man with a no-nonsense demeanor, introduced himself as Detective Michaels. He explained that they had been instructed to take over the case by someone higher up and that they would be handling it from there on out.

Justin was still unsure of what was happening, but Detective Michaels handed him a document that said the Atlanta Police Department would be taking over the case, and no further action was required from him.

"I don't understand," Justin said, looking at the document. "Who instructed you to take over?" He felt Courtney place her hand on his arm in support.

Detective Michaels looked at him gravely. "We were instructed by Mr. Jacob Blakeson," he said. "Maureen's father."

Justin's eyes widened in surprise. He knew that Maureen came from a wealthy family, but he didn't expect them to have this kind of pull.

"What's going to happen now?" he asked.

The other officer, a woman with short blonde hair and a kind face, stepped forward. "We're going to handle it," she said. "You won't hear from Maureen again, and there won't be any record of this."

Justin looked at them skeptically. "What do you mean? How can you make it go away?"

Detective Michaels crossed his arms. "Let's just say that Maureen's father has a lot of influence," he said. "He's handling it, and we're just here to make sure everything goes smoothly."

Justin wasn't sure he liked the sound of that. He had always been a law-abiding citizen and believed in justice being served. But at the same time, he was relieved that Maureen wouldn't be bothering him anymore.

The Atlanta officers explained that he and Courtney didn't need to do anything further and they would be in touch if they needed anything from them. Justin was left feeling both relieved and uneasy about the situation.

As the Atlanta officers left, Courtney turned to Justin and asked, "Are you okay?"

He looked shaken but nodded. "I just can't believe she would do something like this. And to think her father had to get involved…."

Courtney put her arm around him, offering what comfort she could. "It's over now. Let's just try to put it behind us and move on."

JUSTIN LEFT to go get them some food while Courtney held down the fort. The news of what happened with Justin's ex-wife at his shop had spread like wildfire in the town of Sweetgum. Courtney could hear people talking as they passed by, and the phone at the shop kept ringing off the hook with curious customers.

Courtney cleared off the table in the workshop now, carefully setting his tools on the bench where he preferred them. She also made sure to wipe down the table with a clean rag and email that file to their Japanese buyer. She was about to respond to an inquiry about an estimate when she heard the front door jingle.

"Ah, that took a minute," she called out, getting up from her desk. To her shock and amusement, it wasn't Justin.

"What took a minute?" Neveah asked, smirking at her from the doorway.

"Where's the owner? I demand to speak to your manager," Joanne waved.

"Hey, guys!" Courtney said, stepping out from behind the counter to greet them.

"You guys are impossible," Brandi winked, sauntering up to the counter where Courtney stood. "Bad timing?"

"We were about to have lunch," Courtney explained, unsure where Justin had gone off to. Mrs. Zhang was undoubtedly keeping him occupied with chatter.

"Ah, we saw him walk into Mrs. Zhang's place next door," Joanne nodded, looking around the shop. "This place never fails to astound me."

It was a relief to finally have a moment of peace with her friends. She smiled warmly at them, grateful for their visit. "What brings you here?"

"We just wanted to make sure you're okay," Nevaeh said, giving her a hug. "We heard what happened with Justin's ex-wife and wanted to check in."

Courtney appreciated the concern. "I'm fine, really," she assured them. "It was just a little scary."

"I can't believe something like that happened in our town," Brandi said, shaking her head. "Nothing exciting ever happens here."

"I know, right?" Joanne agreed. "This is going to be the talk of the town for years."

Courtney chuckled. "I'm sure it will be," she said. "But let's not dwell on that. How are you guys doing?"

They chatted for a while, catching up on each other's lives and making small talk. Courtney was glad for the distraction, and it was nice to have a moment of normalcy amidst the chaos.

Just then, the bell over the door jingled, and Justin walked in. He looked relieved to see Courtney's friends there.

"Hey, guys," Justin said, smiling at them. "Thanks for stopping by."

"Justin, these are my friends Nevaeh and Brandi." Courtney introduced.

Nevaeh waved and smiled while Brandi gave him a nod. "Nice to meet you," they said in unison.

Joanne grinned at Justin from her spot near the counter. "I see you've already met me," she said with a laugh.

Justin chuckled. "Yeah, you beat them to it."

Courtney stepped closer to him. "These are my closest friends," she said, looking between them. "They just stopped by to make sure I'm okay after everything that happened."

Justin nodded, seeming to understand. "I appreciate that," he said, looking at them. "It's been a crazy day."

Nevaeh and Brandi both nodded, and they all fell into a comfortable conversation about the events of the day. Justin was appreciative of their kindness and enjoyed getting to know them better. He knew that he had made the right decision in coming to Sweetgum and opening up his shop here.

They chatted for a few minutes longer before Nevaeh,

Brandi, and Joanne said their goodbyes and left the shop. As they walked out, Courtney could hear them still talking about the incident.

Courtney looked at Justin, her eyes filled with concern. "I know the town will keep talking about it, but let's not give your ex the satisfaction of being a topic of conversation between us. We need to move past this and focus on the good things in our lives." She reached out and took his hand, giving it a reassuring squeeze.

He smiled down at Courtney fondly and squeezed her hand in return. "Sounds like a plan."

CHAPTER FOURTEEN

*J*ustin leaned back in his chair, taking a sip from his beer. The guys' night had been a long time coming, and he was glad to finally be able to catch up with his friends. Demetrius had closed down the comic book store for the night, and they had the whole place to themselves.

Justin, Demetrius, Sean, and Nate were already good friends with each other. Chris was Nate's good friend and was recently back in town for good after spending several years completing his schooling.

"So Chris, tell us about your Ph.D.," Nate said, shuffling the deck of cards.

Chris smiled, taking a sip of his own beer. "Well, I focused on library sciences and the African-American contribution to the field. It was really interesting, and I feel like I learned so much that I was able to implement at the Sweetgum Library."

Sean, the owner of the local dance studio, leaned forward, intrigued. "That's really cool. What kind of contributions did you find?"

Chris launched into an animated explanation, and the others

listened intently, asking questions and making comments. Justin was glad to see everyone getting along so well.

As they played poker and board games, they briefly mentioned what had happened with Justin's ex-wife at the shop earlier that week. But they quickly moved on to more interesting things, like Nate's latest political ambitions, Demetrius' new comic book recommendations, and Sean's upcoming dance recital.

The guys were all different, but they had a shared history and a love for Sweetgum. As the night wore on and the laughter continued, Justin felt grateful for these friendships.

"Hey, you guys want to try out the new virtual reality headset I just got for the shop?" Demetrius asked, gesturing to a corner of the store.

Everyone agreed eagerly, and they took turns trying out the virtual reality games. Chris was particularly impressed, having never tried VR before.

After a couple of hours playing, they migrated back over to the tables just to relax and talk as Demetrius went to put all the equipment and games away.

"So, how's work?" Nate asked Justin.

"You hired someone to work sales, didn't you?" Sean questioned, running his hand over his hair before grabbing up a beer. "I didn't know you were looking to hire."

"I wasn't," Justin admitted, sipping on his bottle of lager. "But she is one hell of a saleswoman and a real magician when it comes to customer service."

"So, tell us about your new employee," Sean insisted, smirking at Justin as he sipped his beer. "Who is she? How did you meet?"

"I already know all this, but I'd love an update," Nate encouraged, leaning forward.

"Her name is Courtney; she's from Sweetgum," Justin shrugged, trying not to go into too many details.

"Oh, I know her," Chris nodded. "She's friends with my fiancé, Brandi."

"And with India's sister, Neveah," Nate added.

"I met Neveah," Justin nodded, remembering the three women who had come into his shop just the day before. "Courtney's friends seem nice."

"And what about Courtney?" Sean asked, smirking sideways at his friend who sat next to him on the couch. "Does she also seem nice?"

"I know where you're trying to go with this, and I'm not amused," Justin responded, his voice tight.

"I just went through a breakup, and one of my best friends, an incredible guy, has the opportunity to mend his clearly shredded heart," Nate protested, talking straight to Justin. "And he won't even take the chance?"

"It's been years," Sean nodded, seeing Justin's face fall. "Couldn't you at least consider the possibility that there is someone out there for you?"

"There was someone, but she didn't want me in the end," Justin retorted, sipping his beer.

"Psycho," Nate coughed subtly into his hand, and Sean and Chris burst into laughter.

"I'll admit, I really like Courtney, but I don't know that it can go any further than it is. She's my employee and we're friends. That might have to be enough."

"Sounds like you did that on purpose," Nate sighed, taking a larger drink from his bottle. "Subconscious or not, you've put yourself into a corner."

"Thank you, Doctor Phil," Justin retorted, his eyes narrowing.

"Hey, we're just trying to help," Sean interjected, waving his hand. "In case you haven't noticed, we're all hopelessly single and slightly jaded."

"Slightly is an understatement," Justin grumbled, finishing his beer, and grabbing another from the table in front of him.

"Not me," Chris smirked. "I'm happily affianced."

Justin smiled at Chris' declaration. "I'm slowly getting over it, and I do admit that Courtney is helping. She's nothing like Maureen. But, what Maureen did, it broke something in me," Justin admitted, taking a large gulp of beer. "And something like that fundamentally changes you."

Demetrius paused on the way over to them, then disappeared into the backroom.

"I can't even imagine…" Chris said, sipping his beer.

"No, you can't because it is unimaginable," Justin sighed, taking another drink. "I was in love, totally, fully, devoted to her to the point of complete submission. I'd have given her anything and everything."

"That's what love does," Sean sighed.

"I trusted her with everything, I gave my all, and in the end, I was just used," Justin shrugged.

Demetrius came back from the back room carrying a tray of brandy with five glasses. "I think this topic of conversation needs something a little stronger," he said, placing the tray on the table.

"But, she was a user," Nate explained. "She was always looking for the next best thing."

"The bigger, better deal," Justin nodded, finishing his beer. "And she found it."

"She changed you, as intense breakups do," Nate sighed, pouring them each a small glass of brandy. "But, does her influence, her actions, deserve to be reflected onto someone that you're clearly in love with?"

"Love?" Justin laughed, taking the glass of brandy. "We barely know one another…."

"Fine, but does your relationship with Courtney have to be

defined by your past traumas and trust issues?" Nate asked, handing Sean his glass.

"No," Justin sighed, shaking his head. "Courtney is nothing like…."

"Don't say her name," Sean sighed, taking a sip of brandy. "But if she's different, then you owe her the courtesy of treating her differently."

"She's wonderful," Justin sighed, taking a large drink from the glass, almost finishing it. "She's kind, observant, passionate, and genuine, which is more than I can say for my ex."

"And you're afraid of what, exactly?" Demetrius asks.

"I'm afraid that I'll be hurt again, of course," Justin groaned, leaning back in the chair. Staring up at the fluorescent lights as he considered his own emotions.

"Well, you can be afraid, run from your feelings, and probably end up miserable like me," Nate offered, smirking over his glass. "Or, you can take a risk, put yourself out there, and potentially be rewarded a thousand-fold. What other options do you have?"

"That was actually really insightful," Sean admitted, raising his glass. "Who knew!"

"Hilarious," Nate smiled. "So, how do you feel about her? Truly?"

"I want to know more. I want to be around her more than what I already am, which is every day," he groaned, Nate pouring him one more drink. "I want her to like me, and I want to fix that damn watch she commissioned me for."

"Oh?" Chris asked, glancing at Justin. "Watch?"

"A pocket watch, old, belonged to her…uhm, ancestor," Justin smiled, taking another sip of brandy. "But it's so old it is unfixable. I can't find parts or similar watches, and my suppliers and antique dealers are no help. I want so badly to fix it for her, but even my skills aren't up to par for that kind of job. I've considered all I can do, and the only thing left is to go all in and rebuild the watch from the ground up."

"Then do it," Sean encouraged, smiling widely. "What better way to say how you feel for her?"

"You think?" Justin asked, eyes wide. "Really?"

"How have you not considered this?" Nate laughed, raising his glass. "Rebuild the damn watch and surprise her with it. If she doesn't fall into your arms madly in love after that, then she's the idiot, not you."

"No, he's still an idiot," Sean smirked, nudging his now drunk friend. "But at least he's an idiot who can finally admit his feelings for his employee."

"Oh, what if she won't date me because I'm technically her boss?" Justin asked, panic in his slurred words. "I don't want things to get awkward at the shop...."

"One step at a time, my friend," Sean sighed, wrapping an arm around his shoulders. "One step at a time."

"To Courtney, the minx who finally got Justin out of his two-year single slump," Nate smirked, raising his glass. "Cheers, gents."

"Cheers!"

CHAPTER FIFTEEN

The girl's night at Courtney's was fun, Nevaeh, Joanne, and Brandi all enjoying the theme Courtney had come up with. It'd been a while since she felt free like this. She'd decided they'd have some wine, relax, and follow a Bob Ross tutorial for fun. She gave them cheap canvases, lots of oil paints, and their own sets of brushes and palettes. It was so fun, the four setting up in the small living room and opening a bottle of their favorite red.

Courtney sat in her chair, surrounded by her best friends as they all sipped on glasses of red wine and followed along with the Bob Ross tutorial on the TV. It was Courtney's idea to have a girl's night and paint together after finding out that Justin and his friends were having the equivalent.

"This is so much fun, Courtney," Nevaeh said, smiling as she dipped her brush into the paint. "I've never painted before, but I feel like Bob Ross is a natural teacher."

Brandi was also enjoying herself, but her mind seemed to keep drifting to thoughts of her fiance Chris. "I'm so excited about my relationship with Chris," she said, putting down her brush for a moment. "He's just so amazing and we have so much in common."

"Like what?" Nevaeh asked, intrigued.

"Well, Chris is really passionate about writing. He's always been a great writer, and now he's finally taking the time to focus on it. He's even working on writing his own book!" Brandi exclaimed, her eyes shining with pride.

Joanne, who was busy painting away, rolled her eyes. "I'm just too busy for love right now," she said, her brush strokes quick and confident. "I've got my career to focus on and I just don't have the time or energy for a relationship. But, I'm cheering all of you on and will live vicariously through you."

Nevaeh, who was always the life of the party, just shrugged and took a sip of her wine. "I'm all about having fun," she said. "I'm not ready to settle down just yet."

As they continued to paint, the conversation shifted and the four friends chatted and laughed, enjoying each other. Courtney sat back in her chair, listening intently as her best friends discussed their relationships and what they were looking for in potential partners.

"I just want someone who makes me feel special, you know?" Nevaeh said, taking a sip of her wine. "Someone who makes me feel like I'm the only person in the room."

Brandi nodded in agreement. "Yeah, and I want someone who is ambitious and driven. Chris is brilliant and he has a Ph.D., and I just love that about him. He's always pushing himself to do better, and it's inspiring to be around him. You all know how much I love Sweetgum Library, so it should be no surprise that I ended up engaged to the librarian," she giggled.

Nevaeh smiled at Brani and rolled her eyes at Joanne. "You can't just focus on building your coffee empire, Jo. You need to find someone who makes you happy, who you can come home to after a long day and relax with.

Brandi nodded. "And when you do find that person, it will

all be worth it. You'll see how much better your life is with them in it."

Courtney sat quietly, taking in the conversation. She was always fascinated by what her friends were looking for in a relationship, and she was especially interested in this discussion.

Nevaeh turned to her. "What about you, Courtney? What do you want in a partner?"

Courtney shrugged, feeling a little self-conscious. "I don't know. I guess I just want someone who makes me happy and loves me for who I am."

"Let's all just pretend that little Courtney here doesn't already know exactly what she wants in a relationship. She already knows who." Joanne cackled, and the other girls burst into a laughing agreement as Courtney swatted them all lightly with her hand.

"Okay, Courtney, spill it," Nevaeh said, giving her a mischievous grin. "What's going on with you and Justin?"

Courtney sighed, feeling her cheeks flush with heat. Justin was more than the owner of the local watch repair shop where she worked. Over time she had developed feelings for him that went beyond friendship and a working relationship, and she wasn't sure how to face this, let alone tell her best friends.

"Well, you all know it all started when he tried to fix an irreparable watch that's also a family heirloom," Courtney said, her voice soft. "I started spending more time with him, helping him with his books and organizing his orders, and before I knew it, I was falling for him. I know I shouldn't be so ready to jump into something with him, but we're just so effortless...."

Her friends all nodded, their eyes shining with excitement.

"That sounds amazing, Courtney," Brandi said. "Why haven't you told us before?"

"I don't know," Courtney said, shrugging. "I guess I was afraid of ruining the friendship and our working relationship.

That and I wasn't really sure how I felt until very recently, and I'm still not sure how he feels."

"Nonsense," Nevaeh said, waving her hand dismissively. "If you feel something for him, you should tell him. Life is too short to not take chances."

Joanne nodded in agreement. "She's right, Courtney. You never know what could happen if you don't take a chance. Besides, you have to be brave, bold… like your art!"

"Yes!" Brandi exclaimed, smiling widely as she turned from her own somewhat cartoonish painting. "Be bold; tell him how you feel!"

"They are pushy, but right," Nevaeh smirked, staring at her very abstract painting. "But we're right."

As her friends continued to encourage her, Courtney found herself coming to terms with what she wanted. She did have feelings for Justin, and she wanted it to be so much more than just a friendship and a working relationship. He was more than she could have expected, and she had been trying so hard to guard against it. She knew she was attracted from the beginning, but to let herself fall, knowing what would happen, or could happen, was frustrating.

Courtney didn't want to give in to it and yet she did, a bit desperate for the connection. She should have been focusing on other things in her free time, not Justin. She should have been painting and marketing her art online like Kim had done with her hairstyles and braids. She needed to get it out, to free up her time to focus on what should really matter to her. If she told him, she could at least stipulate her terms, her needs, and find out what he wanted and needed.

"Okay," Courtney said, taking a deep breath. "I'll talk to him and at least try to tell him how I feel."

To her surprise, her friends all cheered, clapping her on the back and congratulating her. Joanne started pouring more wine, Brandi was almost screaming, hugging her, and Nevaeh was taking pictures with a knowing smirk. They were always so encouraging, and Courtney wished she'd have said something sooner. She also wished she understood her feelings a bit better.

After another bottle between the four of them, the group began to wind down.

"This was such a great idea, Courtney," Nevaeh said, admiring her finished painting with a giggle from the couch. "I can't wait to do this again."

"Me, too," Brandi agreed, her words slightly slow. "But next time, let's make sure to invite Chris. I'm sure he'd love to join us."

"To a girls' night?" Nevaeh asked,

"No," Joanne insisted, wrinkling her nose.

"Agreed," Courtney said, smiling as she looked around at her friends. "We'll make it a regular thing, but just us girls."

THE NEXT DAY, Courtney was surrounded by the warm, familiar atmosphere of a typical family gathering at Brandi's place. Brandi's boyfriend Chris and Chris's friend Nate were also there. Courtney felt a little nervous around Nate, knowing that he knew Justin quite well. The thought of them talking about her made her feel self-conscious.

However, the atmosphere was too merry and light-hearted for Courtney to dwell on her nerves for long. The sounds of laughter and the smell of good food filled the air as families gathered to enjoy one another. The cookout was being held in Brandi's family's backyard and the sun was shining down on the group of almost thirty people.

Naturally, Nate and Courtney found themselves talking together and it didn't take long for the conversation to turn to Justin. Nate was trying to tease out how Courtney felt about him, but she was too clever to give anything away.

"So, Courtney, how's life at the watch shop?" Nate asked with a charming smile.

"It's good. Busy as usual," Courtney replied, keeping her tone neutral.

"And how's Justin? I hear he's got a real talent for making custom pieces," Nate continued, trying to probe further.

"Yeah, he's definitely talented. His clients are always happy with the work he does," Courtney answered, still being cagey.

Nate chuckled. "You're not giving me much to work with here, Courtney. But I get it; you don't want to say too much about your boss."

Courtney was relieved that Nate had given up on trying to get information out of her. She liked Justin's friend, finding him to be kind and personable, but she also thought he was a little too smooth.

As they continued to chat, Courtney's thoughts kept drifting back to Justin. She thought about how much she admired him and how she wished their relationship could be something more than just a working one.

Love must have been in the air, or else she was noticing it more because of her own feelings, because she noticed Brandi and Chris were having their own conversation discussing their relationship and what they wanted in a partner. They were quietly whispering loving things in each other's ears between family interactions. Joanne was listening to Nevaeh talk about her desires in a relationship, still inspired by the Friday night before.

The gathering continued on in its merry way, with the sounds of laughter and good-natured teasing filling the air. Despite her reservations about Nate, she was glad to be surrounded by people who cared about her and her happiness.

As the day went on, the conversation between Nate and Courtney continued, with Nate asking Courtney more about

Justin. The two of them laughed and talked about their shared experiences with Justin.

"So, what do you think of Justin?" Nate asked, not for the first time, his tone playful.

Courtney smiled, figuring she would throw him a bone. "I think he's great. He's really talented, and he's always so kind to everyone. Plus, he's got a great sense of humor."

"I can tell you like him," Nate said, winking at her.

"You are being nosey. And besides, he's nice, but it's not just that," Courtney said, feeling the need to defend herself. "I mean, he's got a good heart, and he works so hard. I admire that about him."

"I see," Nate said, looking thoughtful. "Well, I can tell you that he's a good guy. He's always been there for me, even when I needed help the most."

Courtney nodded, feeling a sense of pride in Justin. She knew that he was a good guy, but it was nice to hear it from someone else who knew him well. As the evening went on, the conversation shifted to other topics, with Brandi and Chris talking about their plans for the future and Joanne and Nevaeh discussing their jobs. But Courtney thought about Justin and the way her heart skipped a beat every time she did. It was annoying and exhilarating.

The sun began to set, casting a warm glow over the gathering. The families gathered around the picnic tables, and Courtney watched as children laughed and played together, their parents looking on with smiles on their faces. The atmosphere was one of joy and happiness, and Courtney was glad to be surrounded by the community of families.

Brandi's grandmother, Chris's, and all the older women in the community stopped by after church that afternoon and were gone by now, but the other families, and their kids, seemed to make the whole scene light up. The happiness in the faces and voices as the food was partitioned, separated, and packed away for takeaway was what made her love Sweetgum that much more. She knew that was how Justin felt about this place as well. He wasn't from here, but he loved it all the same.

As the night wound down and the families said their goodbyes, Courtney found herself walking back to her car with a smile on her face. She couldn't wait to see Justin again, to work with him, and to be near him. She knew that her feelings for him were growing stronger every day, and she felt excited about what the future might hold.

CHAPTER SIXTEEN

Justin had been thinking about Courtney a lot lately. He loved her creativity and determination, and the way she handled people. He spent an inordinate amount of time watching her while they worked. She walked over, distracting him from his reverie.

"Hey Justin, have you had any orders from overseas lately?" Courtney asked, leaning on the counter.

"Yeah, I actually just got a big one from Japan. They're looking for some rare and antique pieces," Justin replied, trying to keep his focus on the conversation and not on Courtney's playful smile.

"That's so cool! I've always wanted to visit Japan. Have you ever been?" Courtney asked.

"I visited Tokyo when I was in college, and it was amazing. The culture and the history are just incredible," Justin said, smiling at the memories. "It's beautiful, fun, and Tokyo is one of the largest city in the world," Justin explained, happy to talk about where one of his favorite return customers was from.

They continued their conversation, talking about their hobbies and interests and how they both loved the idea of travel. Justin felt like he could talk to Courtney for hours and never run out of things to say.

"Hey Justin, do you have plans for Founders Day in Sweetgum?" Courtney asked, twirling a pen between her fingers.

"It's coming up and I'm pretty excited. I usually donate some of my older pieces, you know? Why? You're going, right?" Justin replied, trying to keep his tone casual.

"Definitely. I love a good street festival. How about you?" Courtney asked, looking up at him with a smile. "Want to meet up?"

"I'll be there. It'll be nice to have a little time off and enjoy the festivities," Justin said, feeling nervous but excited about the possibility of spending more time with Courtney.

They had officially made plans to meet up during Founders Day and Justin felt like it was a sign of things to come. He liked Courtney more and more every day and he was determined to show her just how much she meant to him. He hoped that during the festival they might get a chance to really find out what the other wanted. Justin's hesitation and the thoughts of his past and his ex-wife were always in the back of his mind and he was trying desperately to push it away completely. He didn't want his past to define his future.

***

COURTNEY STOOD NERVOUSLY in front of the mirror, adjusting the straps on her sundress. Today was Founders Day in Sweetgum, and she was meeting up with Justin. She had been looking forward to this day but more so since they made plans to spend it together officially. She wanted everything to be perfect. She had dressed up, hoping to show off her flirty side, but she also wanted to keep things casual.

She had to consider what she wanted from him and how she was going to communicate her feelings, something she feared she wouldn't be good at. She was in her head as she walked towards the community center and when she saw Justin approaching, she paused, waving to him with a soft smile. The main street was buzzing, cut off from traffic and cars, full of people from the town who took the entire day off to enjoy their town's rich history and tradition.

Banners, flags, flowers, and all sorts were strung all through the main drag, the brick and stone buildings beautifully reflected in the large store windows. Courtney loved it and watched Justin approach with a mix of anxiety and anticipation. He was dressed in a casual button-down shirt and jeans, and he had a big smile on his face.

"Hi, Courtney," Justin said, approaching her. "Waiting long?"

"Hey, Justin," Courtney replied, her nerves settling as she took in his smile. "No, I just got here…"

They walked towards the community center, where some of Justin's antiques in the exhibits were set up. They explored the displays, learning about the history of Sweetgum and chatting about the town and their lives in it.

"It's always so fascinating," Courtney admitted, having heard the stories many times over her life. "It never gets old."

"It's rare to have this kind of connection to the past and a community," Justin admitted, nodding at the displays of local history, crafts, art, and photography of what the town used to look like. It had evolved quite a lot since photographs had started in the late 1890s.

As Courtney and Justin walked through the exhibits at the Sweetgum Founder's Day celebration at the community center, they stole glances at each other and share flirty smiles.

"I have to admit, I'm a bit nervous," Courtney said, gesturing to her landscape painting on display. "What if everyone hates it?"

Justin chuckled. "I have no doubt that it's going to be a hit. Your talent is undeniable."

Courtney flushed at his compliment. "Thanks. I like to think I bring a unique perspective to classical landscapes. A little bit of modern, a little bit of abstract."

Justin nodded in agreement. "And it works so well. I'm so proud of you."

As they continued their tour of the exhibits, they came across Justin's antiques from his watch shop on display for the community. He beamed with pride.

"It's amazing to see my work appreciated by this town," Justin said, smiling at Courtney. "I wasn't born and raised in Sweetgum, but it feels like home now."

"I love how passionate you are about your work and this community," Courtney said, placing a hand on his arm. "It's so inspiring."

The two of them continued to walk and talk, admiring the various displays. As they walked away from the exhibit, Justin turned to Courtney and said, "By the way, you look amazing today."

Courtney felt a warm flush creep up her cheeks. "Thank you," she replied with a shy smile.

Justin grinned, "Just stating the truth," he said playfully, nudging her shoulder with his.

As they passed by a particularly impressive sculpture, Justin leaned in close to Courtney and whispered, "I think we make a pretty great team, don't you?"

Courtney's heart skipped a beat and she turned to him with a shy smile. "I couldn't agree more."

Justin smiled back at her and took a step closer, his hand brushing hers. Courtney's heart raced at his touch, and she felt a sense of excitement and anticipation.

For a moment, they stood there, their eyes locked in a silent conversation. Courtney could feel the tension between them growing, and she knew that a kiss was imminent.

Just as Justin leaned in, their lips mere inches apart, they were interrupted by a group of their friends calling out to them.

"You two are too much," came a familiar voice, Brandi and Chris smirking at them from the library display where old books, local authors, genealogy displays, and old historical society photos were highlighted.

Courtney felt a pang of disappointment as Justin stepped back, his eyes still fixed on hers. "Looks like we'll have to finish this conversation later," he whispered with a wry smile.

Courtney nodded, trying to hide the disappointment in her voice. "Yeah, I guess so."

"You look quite cozy," Chris grinned, glancing at Brandi knowingly. "Having fun?"

"Of course, but what about you two?" Courtney asked, shifting the focus to them. "This is a great display! I remember last year's when Everly had these huge records blown up and displayed for the entire town to see."

Justin's hand slipped away from hers, and Courtney felt a sense of longing as she watched him interact with their friends. She wondered what he was thinking and if he felt the same way she did. But she didn't want to push too hard or make things awkward between them.

"Those are at our stall on Main Street," Chris nodded, smiling. "Granny is manning that exhibit, so watch out. She'll tell you all you'd ever need to know…"

"Stop it; she loves the historical society and the records," Brandi smiled, nudging him playfully. "Go, enjoy it; she'd be thrilled to see you both."

"We definitely will," Justin nodded, glancing over the books on display. "I had no idea we had so many local authors and poets."

"Sweetgum inspires the best!" Brandi affirmed, Chris agreeing wholeheartedly.

"Soon to be one more, I hear…"

"Oh, I'm just dabbling," Chris smiled shyly, Brandi smirking at him.

"He's fantastic," she encouraged, Chris kissing her forehead.

"I can't wait to read your work," Courtney said.

"Go, go before I get an ego," Chris dismissed, his arm around Brandi's waist as another group of locals approached the display. Courtney and Justin waved goodbye.

As they strolled through the exhibits, Courtney and Justin's eyes met, and they exchanged a long, lingering gaze. Justin's hand brushed against Courtney's as they walked, and she felt a jolt of electricity shoot through her.

Courtney smiled at him, and Justin grinned back, their shoulders bumping playfully. "You're having a good time, right?" Justin asked, looking at her with a mischievous glint in his eye.

Courtney nodded, her smile growing wider. "Of course, I am," she replied, "but it's even better because I'm here with you."

Justin's eyes lit up at her words, and he leaned in closer to her. "I feel the same way," he said, his voice low and husky.

Courtney's heart skipped a beat as Justin's hand brushed against hers again. She couldn't wait to explore this new territory between them, but for now, they continued to flirt and playfully tease each other, enjoying the company and the moment.

They finished the last few displays, heading to the large double doors and made their way to the local shops on Main Street, admiring the shop owners' booths for the celebration. They tried the food from Rochelle's, Joanne's, and Mrs. Zhang, feeling absolutely stuffed as they made their way back up the main street. There were even small fundraisers featuring games, the two playing with laughter.

They met friends and families of the town here as well, becoming distracted or sidetracked into conversations they both enjoyed greatly. Everly even stopped them, telling Justin all about some of the local history and how his pieces from the shop, antiques, and random objects, played a part in the town's development.

As Courtney and Justin walked down Main Street, they ran into familiar faces, including Rochelle, who beamed at the sight of them. "Well, look at you two lovebirds! Enjoying Founder's Day, I see."

Justin chuckled, "Of course, Rochelle. This is a great day for the community."

Mrs. Zhang and her husband walked by and greeted them with a warm smile. As they continued their walk, they ran into Demetrius. Courtney knew Justin and Demetrius were friends, but she had never really talked to Demetrius much.

"Hey man, how's the comic scene today?" Justin asked.

"Oh, you know, just promoting some new releases. And who's this?" Demetrius asked, looking towards Courtney.

"This is Courtney; she's a local artist," Justin introduced.

"Nice to meet you, Courtney."

"Nice to meet you, too," she smiled, picking up a graphic novel from his exhibit.

"Graphic novels, huh? I can introduce you to the concept if you're interested."

"This art style is really interesting," Courtney smiled, opening the novel. "And sure, I'm always open to trying new things."

As they continued talking about the graphic novels, the conversation was light and fun and highlighted their surroundings and the community celebrating the holiday. Justin and Demetrius shared their love for comics, and Courtney was pleasantly surprised by the humor and wit in their discussion.

"You know, I can see why you two are such good friends," Courtney said, laughing.

"Yeah, we just have the same kind of humor," Demetrius replied, playfully shoving Justin.

The three of them continued their conversation, admiring

the sights and sounds of the community coming together for Founder's Day. It was a while later that Justin and Courtney finally left the display, Courtney purchasing the graphic novel she had been admiring. Demetrius also sent her an email list of graphic novel styles and stories she might also be interested in.

A HALF-HOUR LATER, after they grabbed something to drink from Joanne's café, they wandered into the park. As the sun began to set, Courtney and Justin found themselves walking along the paths and shaded ways, smiling at each other while families and children began to pack up and move toward the main event space, a stage in the park where a local band and speakers were gathering.

Courtney and Justin weren't paying much attention. They talked about the sights and sounds of the day and the excitement of the Founders Day celebration. Justin was intrigued by Courtney's passion for history and how she had taken a great interest in the stories and legends of the town of Sweetgum. She told him about her favorite parts of the day and the quirky little shops and games they had visited.

As they stopped to sit on a bench near the blooming community garden, the tension between them grew palpable. They were both nervous, unsure of what to say or do next. But then, without warning, they found themselves leaning in towards each other, their faces mere inches apart. Just as they were about to share their first kiss, the sound of someone clearing their throat behind them interrupted them. Again.

They turned to see Nate standing there with a wide grin on his face. "Well, well, well, what do we have here?" he said in a teasing tone. "It looks like love is in the air!"

Courtney and Justin both laughed nervously, Courtney feeling embarrassed at being caught and irritated by the interruption. They chatted with Nate for a while, and after her irritation wore off, she began enjoying his stories and laughter.

They eventually parted ways with Nate and made their way back to the stage area. As the evening continued, they found themselves flirting more and more, and the tension between them was palpable.

When it was time to say their goodbyes, Courtney did so with disappointment for the two missed opportunities and hope for what the future might hold.

CHAPTER SEVENTEEN

As Courtney walked through the bustling streets of Sweetgum, her thoughts were consumed with Justin. Their day together on Founder's Day had been perfect, filled with flirty banter and nonstop laughter. She thought about the two almost-kisses they had shared before they were interrupted. The memory still made her heart flutter with excitement.

She wondered if Justin felt the same way about her. He was always so hard to read, but she had a feeling that he was just as into her as she was into him. Courtney had been trying to be patient, waiting for him to make the first move, but her nerves were starting to get the best of her. She just wanted to know where they stood because the weekend had passed with no further communication, and she felt confused. Was she imagining everything that happened?

Just as she was lost in thought, her phone rang. It was Nevaeh.

"Hey, just wanted to check in on you after you spent Founder's Day with Justin," Nevaeh said, excitement in her voice.

"Yeah, it was amazing but also frustrating," Courtney said with a sigh.

"Why frustrating? You guys had a great time together, right?" Nevaeh asked, curious.

"We did, but every time I thought he was going to make a move, we were interrupted," Courtney explained, her frustration evident in her voice.

"Wait, what do you mean he was going to make a move?" Nevaeh asked, shocked.

"I mean, we were getting close, our faces were inches apart, and then, *bam*, interruption," Courtney explained, a hint of disappointment in her voice.

"Okay, girl, you need to stop being a chicken and make your move," Nevaeh encouraged, "This isn't the old days when women couldn't make a move. You need to take what you want."

"I know, but what if he doesn't feel the same way?" Courtney asked, her nerves showing.

"Have you ever thought about just asking him how he feels?" Nevaeh suggested.

"I don't know, it's just not that easy," Courtney said, feeling uncertain.

"Why not? You guys have a great connection, and from what you've told me, it sounds like he was getting ready to make a move. So, what's stopping you?" Nevaeh asked.

"I don't know, I guess I'm just scared of rejection," Courtney admitted.

"Girl, rejection is just a part of life. But you'll never know what could have been if you don't take a chance. You deserve to be happy, and if Justin is the one who can make you happy, then go for it," Nevaeh encouraged.

"I'm just not as excited as I was…." Courtney admitted, trepidation in her voice.

"What's going on, Courtney? You sound down, and where did your confidence go?" Nevaeh asked.

"We had such a great time on Founder's Day, and I thought maybe something was finally going to happen between us. But since then, nothing's happened. I don't know what to do."

"Don't be a chicken, Courtney," Nevaeh scolded her. "If you want something, you need to go for it. Besides, it's only been two days."

"I know, I know," Courtney replied. "But what if I make a move and he's not interested? That would be so embarrassing."

"What's the worst that could happen?" Nevaeh asked. "At least you'll know where you stand and can move on. Don't let your chance with Justin slip by."

"You're right," Courtney said, her confidence starting to build. "I'll do it. I'm going to march into that watch shop and talk to him."

"That's my girl," Nevaeh cheered. "I have faith in you. You're strong, confident, and beautiful. Just remember, you deserve to be happy."

"Thanks, Nevaeh. You always know how to make me feel better," Courtney said, feeling grateful for her friend's support.

"Anytime, girl. That's what friends are for. Now, go get him!" Nevaeh encouraged.

Courtney's confidence grew with each word of encouragement from Nevaeh. She felt empowered and ready to take control of her love life. When she hung up the phone, she felt a renewed sense of determination. Courtney arrived at the watch shop and went straight to the workshop in the back, where she knew she would find Justin. She had to remind herself that she wanted this. She wanted him. She dropped her things in her small office, checked the register and desk, turned the lights on, and went back to see Justin in his workshop before opening the front door.

As she entered the workshop, she was greeted by the sight of Justin bent over a delicate watch mechanism, his focus completely absorbed in his work. She stood there for a moment, just staring at him, unsure of whether she should launch herself at him or just confess her feelings for him. But before she could make a move, Justin looked up and noticed her standing there.

"Good morning, Courtney," he said, his eyes lighting up.

"Good morning," she replied, smiling.

"I had fun at Founder's Day," Justin smiled, still looking at whatever it was he was working on. "I hope you did, too…"

"I did," she agreed. "It was an almost perfect day."

"Almost…?"

"Well, it was pretty perfect," she corrected, flushing.

"I think so too," he said, glancing over at her, then up at another painting she had brought into the shop. "I think you should display your art at a booth next year for Founder's Day."

"Oh, I couldn't… I'm just mediocre at best."

"That's a lie," he laughed, his lips pulling into a smile. "You can do it; I know it."

"I wish I had your confidence…"

"You can take as much as you want. I sometimes have too much," he smirked, turning to look at her now. "So, what do you think about getting some barbecue for lunch?" Justin asked.

"That sounds great," Courtney said. "I've been craving it all week."

"Good, and I hope the orders aren't overwhelming you," he said, moving to stand. "I know we've had a steady increase lately, so I want to make sure you aren't overwhelmed. after all, it's just you… I was considering hiring a part-timer to help with the paperwork, to be honest."

"No, I can handle it. I enjoy it," Courtney said, not liking the idea of sharing the workday with someone else. She really enjoyed their time together, just the two of them.

They talked about how the exhibits had gone, how busy the shop had been, and how everyone was talking about how much they loved the antique pocket watches on display. Justin lit up at this, Courtney unable to stop her delighted smile.

"I'm so glad people appreciate them as much as I do," Justin said. "I've always had a passion for antiques and being able to share it with the community here in Sweetgum makes it even better."

"I know," Courtney said. "I've always loved your work, and I'm so proud to be a part of it."

Their conversation flowed easily, and it was clear that they had a strong connection. As they talked, Courtney thought about how compatible they were and how much she loved spending time with him.

"I'm so glad we have this time to talk," Justin finally said, as if reading her thoughts. "I feel like we never have enough time to catch up with each other, even though we see and talk to one another every day."

"I know," Courtney said. "But I'm just so happy to be here with you, talking and laughing like this."

And with that, they continued their conversation, lost in their own world and completely at ease with each other. Courtney had almost forgotten about her mission to just tell him her feelings, hoping that the way she said things, and how encouraging she was, would speak for her.

"We better open up," Justin finally smirked, realizing it was well past the time.

"Oh!" Courtney gasped, rushing back out to the shop to unlock the door and change the sign to 'open.'

⁂

As Courtney sat at her small desk an hour later in her office, her thoughts turned once again to love. She had been working at the shop for a little under a month now, and her feelings for Justin had grown stronger with each passing day. Although she hadn't known him that long before starting to work at the shop, it was the close quarters and daily interactions that had truly brought them together.

She couldn't deny it anymore; she was in love with Justin whether he felt the same or not. She admired his passion for his work, his intelligence, and his kind heart. He was so different from anyone she had ever met, and she was glad to have him in her life.

As she sat in her office, surrounded by the familiar sounds of the workshop and the street outside, Courtney daydreamed about a possible future with Justin. She pictured them going on adventures together, exploring new places and trying new things. She envisioned a life full of laughter and love, and she knew that with Justin by her side, anything was possible.

She also thought about the challenges that lay ahead. They had both been hurt in the past and opening up to someone new was always a risk. But she was willing to take that risk for Justin. She wanted to be with him, to be his partner and his support system.

Courtney took a deep breath and leaned back in her chair. She knew that she couldn't wait forever for Justin to make the first move; she had to take control of her own happiness. She was determined to show him how she felt, to let him know that she was ready for a future with him.

As she sat in her office, thinking of Nevaeh's words from that morning, Courtney made a promise to herself. She would work up the courage to tell Justin how she felt, and she wouldn't let anything stand in her way. She was in love with him, and she was going to make sure he knew it.

COURTNEY WALKED into the workshop of the watch shop, a smile on her face, a half hour later. She had received a couple of exciting orders in her emails that day, and she couldn't wait to share them with Justin.

"So far, so good?" she asked, her voice light and cheerful.

Justin looked up from his workbench and smiled back at her. "Going great, Courtney. What's the news? You look like you've got something to say…"

"Well, I got an order for a classic pocket watch from a buyer in New York and another for a stylized piece from a buyer in Seattle," she said, her eyes shining with excitement. "I forwarded the latter email to you so you could take a look."

Justin nodded, a smile playing at the corners of his lips. "Sounds great. I'll take a look at it later today."

Courtney so badly wanted to tell Justin how she felt about him, but she didn't know how to bring it up. As she was about to speak, she noticed that Justin was working on a commission she didn't recognize. She walked closer and realized that it was her family pocket watch. She was speechless, tears welling up in her eyes as she watched the second hand tick away.

"Justin…how did you fix it? I thought it was impossible," she said, her voice shaking with emotion.

"It was supposed to be a surprise," he said, a smile on his face. "But I managed to fix it."

Courtney burst into tears. She hugged him tightly.

"Thank you, Justin. Thank you so much," she said, her voice filled with emotion.

Justin hugged her back, and the two of them stood there for a moment. It was a moment that Courtney would always treasure, a moment that gave her hope for the future she wanted with Justin. It was only when they pulled apart that she looked at the watch itself. He handed it to her carefully, a wide bright smile on his face as she inspected it happily, pushing away tears of joy.

"I wanted to surprise you," Justin said, his own voice soft and gentle. "I know it's not much, but I wanted to do something to show you how much you mean to me."

Courtney smiled through her tears. "It's more than enough. Thank you so much. I don't know what to say."

"You don't have to say anything," Justin replied, his hand coming up to caress her cheek. "I just wanted to do something special for you."

"You always do," Courtney said, leaning into his touch. "You always make me feel special, Justin."

The two of them stood there, lost in the moment until the sound of a customer coming in the front door interrupted them. Courtney quickly wiped her eyes and took a deep breath, trying to compose herself.

"I'll go take care of that," she said, her voice still a bit shaky. "Thank you again, Justin. I don't know what to do without you."

Justin smiled at her and turned back to his workbench. "Let's hope you'll never have to find out," he said softly.

CHAPTER EIGHTEEN

*J*ustin sat in his workshop, lost in thought as he gazed at the intricate inner workings of a pocket watch. His mind was a jumbled mess of emotions, fear, and excitement battling for dominance. He had developed strong feelings for Courtney, and he was terrified of acting further on them. The memory of his ex-wife still haunted him, and the thought of being hurt like that again was too much to bear.

His ex-wife had ruined his trust and broken his heart. The hurt still lingered, and he was afraid of repeating that experience with Courtney. However, he knew she was different. She was kind, smart, and understanding, and he felt like he could truly be himself around her. He had grown to care deeply for her, and that was obvious now, but he was scared of making the wrong move and ruining what they had.

As Courtney dealt with a walk-in customer, Justin's thoughts continued to swirl. He didn't know how to approach this new relationship that was blooming between them. He was nervous and excited all at once, but he also knew that he had to be careful. The past couldn't be repeated, and he had to approach his future with a fresh perspective.

He thought of his friends Nate and Chris, who had been encouraging him all along. They had seen how happy he was around Courtney and urged him to take a chance. Justin knew that they were right, but fear still held him back. He was afraid of opening himself up and getting hurt again, but he was also aware that he couldn't live his life in fear.

As he sat there, lost in thought, Justin realized that he needed to let go of the past and embrace the future. He was ready to take a chance on love and see where it took him, even if it might be painful. He made a promise to himself to be open and honest with Courtney, to give their relationship a chance to blossom, and to not let fear dictate his actions.

With newfound determination, Justin put down the pocket watch and headed toward the front of the shop. As he approached Courtney, he took a deep breath and smiled. He was ready to take a chance and see where this newfound love would take him. However, the unhappy customer in the shop was quite worried.

As Justin joined Courtney at the front of the shop, he noticed that Lyle had returned. Justin listened intently as Lyle spoke of the sentimental value his broken pocket watch held, how it had been passed down from his father, and how much it meant to him.

"It's an old watch, and I try to treat it with care," Lyle said, nodding at them. "But my job can get a bit rough and I like to keep the watch nearby."

"I understand that!" Courtney nodded, encouraging him. "I do that with my own pocket watch."

"Oh, you've got one too?" Lyle asked, curious as he pulled the worn but clean-faced silver piece from his pocket. "Mine's been around for years in my family. I was excited to pass it on to my son and his daughter, but it stopped working a week ago."

"It's beautiful," Courtney nodded, setting out a cloth for Lyle to set the watch on. "Can you tell me more about the history?"

"Her family watch is similar and has a lot of deep meaning and connections," Justin explained, standing next to her for support. "Does your watch have a story too?"

"Oh, many," he laughed, Courtney offering him the stool behind the counter. Justin picked it up, set it on the other side of the counter, and Lyle accepted it happily. "Where to start…"

"When did your family first buy it?" Justin asked, observing the older watch. It was older than Courtney's, which was interesting as hers was from the 1890s. He had worked on the watch before, cleaning and replacing gears, so he already knew the answer. However, he wanted Courtney to hear about Lyle's family heirloom in hopes they could connect over it.

"My great-grandfather purchased it with his first real wage for Christmas in 1869," Lyle nodded, nostalgia across his face. "I remember my grandfather telling me this story as a kid and I thought it was a pretty good gift to buy yourself."

"Can you tell us the story?" Courtney asked, eyes wide. Justin admired her fascination with the history, picking up the watch delicately. He was familiar with it and immediately saw it needed a cleaning.

"Well, my great-great-grandfather, Samuel, had been born on a plantation in the 1840s," Lyle explained, Courtney listening intently. "It wasn't here in Georgia, but over in Mississippi. When he was in his twenties, the Civil War broke out and he was sold to a man who built part of the railroads here in Georgia. He met my great-great-grandmother there, Sarah. Once they were allowed to marry, they did, though it was a bit silly to wait for permission. That was the year that the war ended, only a few months before the surrender."

"Really?" Courtney asked, her bright eyes alight. Justin smiled at this, remembering his reaction to Lyle's story when he first heard it.

"Really," Lyle laughed. "It was a bit ironic but they could have waited and married however they wanted. But Papa Samuel, the second he learned they were freed, moved to Augusta."

"There he spent three years saving from odd jobs, dirty jobs, building themselves a small house just outside the city, in what is actually pretty close to the center today," Lyle nodded, his voice full of pride. "But in their fourth year, when my great-grandfather was two, Papa Samuel got himself a steady long-term career. His experience working on the railroads made him an ideal candidate for railyard foreman."

"He traveled a bit throughout Georgia and the south for a year, saved more money as granny Sarah was pregnant, and that's when he discovered Sweetgum," Lyle sighed, his tone wistful, happy to reminisce. "He came home one day, after being away for three days, and told granny that they were moving. I'd have liked to have been there for that conversation – granny Sarah didn't take no guff from anyone, you know?"

"I like granny Sarah already," Courtney laughed, her wide smile bright as Justin listened while considering Lyle's watch.

"She was close to having her baby, and he wanted to just up and sell their home and move to this tiny town near the mountains," Lyle laughed. "Can you imagine? Naturally, granny wanted to make him wait until the baby was born, and he agreed. He needed to work something out with the rail company, as Augusta and Sweetgum are a long way away from one another, even on a train."

"It had to have been at least a few hours via train," Courtney surmised, thinking about it.

"Long way considering the trains didn't travel as fast as they do now," Lyle nodded. "But sure enough, granny had her second baby, Aunty June, and then they spent one final Christmas in Augusta before moving. It was that Christmas that papa Samuel went to a pretty famous watch maker in Augusta and purchased this very pocket watch."

"Funny thing is, he wanted it to be a gift for himself and his job," Lyle nodded. "But granny Sarah loved the watch just as much, so she kept it safe and at their new home in Sweetgum while he purchased a cheaper one for the railway."

"He was able to keep his rail job?" Courtney asked, Justin smirking as he set the watch back down on the cloth.

"He was; they transferred him to the rail hub just an hour train from Sweetgum," Lyle explained, pointing toward the door. "It's no longer there and got combined with the larger lines in the 1920s, but Papa Samuel worked there for over thirty years."

"That's a beautiful history to have," Courtney gushed, absolutely enthralled. "What about your great-grandpa? When did he get the watch from Granny Sarah?"

"Oh, that's a fun story, too," Lyle laughed, shaking his head.

Justin loved listening to Courtney interact with customers, and Lyle was one of his most fascinating customers. Courtney, who had clearly never properly talked to Lyle until now, was alight with questions and truly fascinated by his family history.

"Well, my great-grandaddy, who I'm named after, was a different man altogether," Lyle reminisced, leaning against the counter with a grimace. "He wanted to move west and left Sweetgum when he was sixteen. Now, you have to remember; this is in the 1880s when there was a big push to the west, before the highways and the cars and all that."

"It must have been extremely dangerous…"

"Well, he was trying to go north first, to Chicago, and then set off for Oregon," Lyle smirked. "But he fell in love in Chicago with my granny, Rosie."

"That's beautiful…"

"He was in Chicago for a year, saving up money, looking to take the first coach he could afford to Saint Louis," Lyle explained, pointing at the watch. "But the watch was still back in Sweetgum with his parents. Well, after meeting Granny

Rosie, he decided he wanted to stay in Chicago and live. He sent for the watch after he proposed to Rosie, and his parents insisted they come down to Sweetgum for the wedding. That's when Papa Samuel gifted the watch to great-grandaddy Lyle."

"And Rosie's family? They come down to Sweetgum for the wedding?"

"Her parents, her two siblings, and their spouses all made the trip down via train," Lyle smirked, winking at her. "Grandaddy Lyle used to always joke that he married into money when he fell in love with granny Rosie."

"They moved back to Chicago then?" Justin asked, chiming in. He hadn't heard this story yet.

"Oh, no, Granny Rosie fell in love with Sweetgum and refused to leave," Lyle laughed, nudging Justin. "Like you!"

"That's so wonderful!" Courtney giggled, placing her hand on her chest. "It's beautiful that they settled here."

"Well, not really settled," Lyle smirked. "My namesake was a wanderer, an explorer of sorts. He and granny Rosie took a train, when my grandpa Johnnie was only five, out west to Saint Louis. They wanted to settle there and did for almost fifteen years, where great-grandaddy worked on a riverboat. He explored the Mississippi, sometimes taking my grandad to places like Baton Rouge or up to Minnesota during long trips. In Louisiana is where grandpa learned to play the guitar."

"Your grandpa played the guitar?" Justin asked, more new information as he and Courtney were equally drawn in.

"Well, yeah, Papa Johnnie was in a blues band for ten years," Lyle laughed, smiling at their reactions. "I could have sworn I told ya this, Justin."

"No, I had no idea, but it's so interesting," he admitted, picking up the watch. "I knew the watch had some history, but this is beyond anything I imagined. This watch has seen some adventures, for sure."

"Oh, papa Johnnie was a real wildcard," Lyle sighed, memories flooding his eyes and face. "I remember him teaching me the guitar when I was little, though I was never good at it. He was full of stories about the riverboats and his travels across the north with his band in Chicago, Detroit, Cincinnati, Memphis…"

"Did they settle back into Sweetgum?" Courtney questioned, her curiosity overwhelming.

"Oh, yeah, Grandaddy Lyle and Rosie moved back to Sweetgum around 1902," he surmised, nodding. "Papa Samuel was ill around that time and only lived a couple more years later, Granny Sarah following a year later. Grandaddy Lyle inherited their house and gifted it to Aunty June, who raised her family there."

"Johnnie met his wife here in Sweetgum, actually," Justin chimed in, remembering this story. "Wasn't it Nate's great-aunt?"

"You've got a good memory," Lyle nodded, smiling at Courtney. "He fell in love with a firecracker of a woman and the aunt of the current mayor."

"Ah, I met Nate, but I only saw the mayor at the Heritage Day festivities…."

"Well, my Grandma Barb made Granny Sarah and Rosie look tame," Lyle smirked, his eyes alight. "She taught me so much, and she was a real character. She was the librarian for years before Everly. And she was very involved with the town history and preservation works, including pushing the state to preserve and protect the state park here in Sweetgum."

"Is that why you became a park ranger?" Courtney asked, almost buzzing with excitement.

"Part of it, yes," he smirked. "But I loved hiking, spending camping trips with my dad, who was in the military."

"One of the first and only black commanders during the Pacific War, right?" Justin remembered, loving this history.

"Oh yeah, my dad was a no-nonsense kind of guy and named

after Papa Samuel," Lyle sighed. "He was a tough but loving man and treated me, my brother John, my sister Rosie, and my mamma June quite well, like we were some sort of royalty.

"Camping trips, fishing, traveling to where our family used to live in Saint Louis and Chicago, and giving us what we thought was the best childhood ever," Lyle nodded. "I'm the oldest, born in 1947, two years after he was stationed here in Georgia at the air force base."

"Thank you for sharing these stories with me," Courtney sighed, her eyes full of emotion. "You have no idea how much I appreciate it. My family history is a bit of a mystery to me, but my own heirloom pocket watch means just as much, and I totally understand your panic over yours. It's such an important piece for your family, so we have to figure out how to get it working again."

Courtney, being the kind and caring person she was, immediately offered to have a look at the watch and see if she could help. Justin saw the determination in her eyes as she took the watch from the counter again and inspected it. She didn't know too much, only what Justin had told her and instructed her to look out for, but she was genuinely concerned for Lyle. After a few moments of examination, she handed the watch over to Justin, telling Lyle that he was a miracle worker.

Feeling a sense of pride, Justin promised Lyle that he would do everything in his power to fix the watch. He could see the relief on Lyle's face as Courtney set up a receipt and a box for him to put the watch in. He admired Courtney's kindness and the way she effortlessly put others at ease, further solidifying his love for her as his mind raced to figure out how to make it plain.

As he considered the broken watch, Justin thought about how lucky he was to have Courtney in his life. Her generosity and caring nature were traits that he had been searching for in a partner for a long time, and he was happy to have found them in her. The moments they shared together, like this one with Lyle, only served to strengthen his feelings for her. He was nervous and excited about their relationship, but he was determined to approach it with a fresh perspective and not let the past repeat itself.

He also remembered the encouragement from his friends Nate, Sean, and Chris, who had been his cheerleaders the whole time. He was thankful for their support and took comfort in the knowledge that he had people in his life who believed in him. He felt optimistic about his future with Courtney, and he couldn't wait to see where this new relationship would lead. As Lyle left the shop, Justin and Courtney both smiled and waved, relieved to have helped another customer. The older man was very grateful, thanking them both as he walked out the door with his receipt in hand.

After Lyle left, Courtney walked over to the shelf in the workshop where she stored the watches that were waiting to be fixed, placing Lyle's watch with the others. Justin followed her, noticing how she picked up her own family heirloom watch, the one that had started ticking again that very day. But instead of smiling, Courtney began to cry. Justin was taken aback, his heart breaking at the sight of her tears. He quickly made his way over to her, taking the watch from her hands and setting it down on his bench.

"What's wrong?" he asked, his voice filled with concern.

As he pulled her into his arms and held her close, he felt a sense of rightness, as if she was meant to be there with him. He peppered kisses on her head, feeling more and more certain with every passing moment that this was where he belonged.

But he couldn't ignore the reason for her tears. So, he gently wiped them away and asked her again, "What's wrong?"

"It's just that I had accepted that the watch was broken," Courtney explained, sniffling. "I had been meaning to ask for it back, just the way it was. Because when I met you, I was broken and unhappy. And now, the watch is fixed, just like me."

Justin felt a wave of guilt wash over him, realizing what he had done. "I'm sorry," he said, "I wanted to show you that I cared. The only skill I have is fixing things."

Courtney looked up at him, a soft smile on her face. "That's okay," she said, "the watch is a symbol of our meeting. It will always remind me of the moment when we first met and everything started to change for the better."

As Justin held Courtney close, he thought about his past relationship and the pain that had come with it.

"Courtney, I want you to know that I'm not perfect. I've been through a tough breakup, and I don't want that to shape my future relationships. I want to be open and honest with you."

Courtney looked up at him, understanding in her eyes. "I understand, Justin. I've been through my own struggles too. I'm not perfect either."

"My ex-wife... she hurt me in ways I can't even fully explain," he whispered, looking into her eyes. "I need you to understand that it shaped me, but it also won't be what shapes my future, especially with you."

"Do we have a future?" she asked, a small smile on her face. He grinned back, kissing her forehead gently.

Justin hugged her tighter, thankful for her understanding and the humor in that moment. "I want you in my life, Courtney. I want us to support each other. Your art, my tinkering, and our relationship while here at the shop could be something magical, I think...."

Courtney smiled and leaned her head against his chest. "I want that too, Justin. I'm so glad we have each other now; I hope you know that. You are more than your trauma and your past is simply memories, something you can and will overcome. I'll help you if I can."

"You're amazing," he whispered, pulling her closer. "I want to cultivate your dreams, Courtney. I want to be there for you and help make them a reality."

Courtney looked up at him with a contented smile and pushed her hair from her cheek. "Thank you, Justin. That means so much to me."

They held each other for a few moments longer, enjoying the comfort of their embrace. He felt like they had found something special in each other, and they were determined to make it work. It was torture when they finally had to separate, Justin feeling a bit disappointed. As they pulled away from each other, Justin looked into Courtney's eyes and spoke from the heart.

"Courtney, I want you to know how much you mean to me. You helped me begin to heal simply by being yourself. I never thought I'd be worthy of love again after my messy marriage and divorce, but you made me see that I am. You embraced my passion for watchmaking and inspired me to be more creative than I have been in years. You need to know that you've given me more than I could have possibly hoped for."

Courtney smiled at Justin." I had no idea you felt this way, Justin. I'm so happy that you want to share this with me. I feel so much closer to you already."

Justin took a deep breath before continuing. "I'm sorry it took me so long to let you know how I feel, and I'm even sorrier that we haven't gone on a date yet. I want to remedy that situation as soon as possible."

"Then you better ask me out!" she joked, hugging him again.

"Fair enough… Will you go out with me?"

"I'll have to consider it," Courtney beamed at Justin, that playful smirk on her face. "Of course, I will! I would love to go out with you."

Justin pulled Courtney into a tight embrace. "I promise you; I'll make it a night to remember."

With a laugh, Justin and Courtney made plans for their first official date. For the first time in a long time, Justin felt like he had a second chance at love.

AS THEY BOTH settled back into their work, Courtney went to her small office next to Justin's workshop. She smiled, thinking about the conversation they just had. She opened her email inbox, but before she could get to work, a message from Justin popped up. It was a funny meme, and she burst out laughing. She quickly replied with a meme of her own, and their banter continued throughout the day.

In between their playful messages, Courtney attended to customer inquiries and updated their social media and adver-tisements. She was still trying to stifle a giggle whenever she saw Justin's messages on her phone or computer. It was a welcome distraction from her work.

MEANWHILE, Justin was focused on his work in the workshop. He was tinkering with Lyle's watch, a simple replacement in his mind. It was a common older model, and he had replaced many of them before. However, as he worked, he smiled when he saw Courtney's messages. He took a quick break to reply with a joke, and their banter continued.

As the day went on, they both found themselves taking more and more breaks to send each other memes and jokes. They laughed and smiled; their chemistry impossible to ignore. But they didn't let it distract them completely, and they still managed to get some work done.

At one point, Justin even came over to Courtney's office to show her a joke he found particularly funny. They laughed and chatted, their faces close together. Justin thought about how lucky he was to have Courtney in his life, and he vowed to never let anything come between them.

As the day ended, Justin closed up the workshop and joined Courtney in her office. They sat together, their legs touching, as they continued their playful banter. Justin leaned in and whispered, "I'm so happy you're here, Courtney."

Courtney smiled. "I feel the same way, Justin. You've made my life so much better, and I'm so glad to have you in it."

Justin couldn't resist any longer. He reached for Courtney's hand, intertwining his fingers with hers, and leaned in to press his lips against hers. The kiss was soft and tender at first but quickly grew more passionate as they explored each other's mouths.

Courtney wrapped her arms around Justin's neck, pulling him in closer. He ran his hands up and down her back, and he felt her shiver.

They broke the kiss, both gasping for breath, their foreheads resting against each other. Justin whispered, "I've wanted to do that for so long, Courtney."

"I know," she replied, her voice filled with desire. "Me, too."

Justin leaned in for another kiss, their lips meeting in a fiery embrace. They lost themselves in the moment, forgetting about the world around them and enjoying their first kiss together.

He was so happy, so unimaginably giddy, that he didn't care if customers walked in on them. He'd continue in front of them, just to make sure everyone knew how happy the two had become.

CHAPTER NINETEEN

Courtney sat at the booth at Rochelle's diner, surrounded by her closest friends and the older women from the book club. Nevaeh, Brandi, and Joanne were all there, along with Mrs. Zhang and Rochelle. The conversation was stimulating, with everyone talking about the latest developments in their lives. But instead of discussing their latest romance novel, *A Duke, A Doily, and A Dilemma: A Regency Romance of Love, Lace, and Laundry*, the topic of conversation was about Courtney and Justin.

Her friends were all gushing about their excitement for their upcoming first date that night. Brandi was talking about how she always knew something would happen between them and how happy she was for them both. Joanne was giving Courtney tips on what to wear while Nevaeh was teasing her about how nervous she was.

Courtney felt her cheeks turn hot as she listened to her friends. She had always been shy about her feelings, but now that they were out in the open, she was a little bit nervous. But she was also excited. She and Justin had been getting closer over the past few days, and she couldn't wait to see where things would go between them after tonight's date.

The older women in the book club were also chiming in, sharing their own stories about finding love later in life. Mrs. Zhang was talking about how she met her husband and how he had always been her rock. Rochelle was reminiscing about her own romantic adventures, which made everyone laugh. Despite the nervousness she felt, Courtney was happy. As they all laughed and chatted, Courtney smiled, knowing that she was exactly where she was meant to be.

The women of the book club continued to chat excitedly, their attention fully on Courtney and her newfound romance with Justin. "I can't believe you're finally dating!" Nevaeh exclaimed, her eyes wide with excitement. "You two have been talking for months now; it's about time!"

Brandi nodded in agreement, sipping on her coffee. "I remember when we came into the shop for the first time, and I just knew there was something special between you two. I'm so happy it's finally happening."

Joanne chimed in, "I agree. Justin is such a sweet guy, and he's obviously head over heels for Courtney. I can tell just by the way he looks at her."

Mrs. Zhang smiled warmly at Courtney, patting her hand. "My dear, you deserve happiness. And I can see that Justin is just the man to give it to you. You're like that married couple when you come to my place for lunch, ordering the same things without even having to ask, right?"

Rochelle nodded in agreement. "Same from here, though they will occasionally change it up when it comes to the fresh pies. And I've known Justin for years now since he moved here, and I've never seen him this happy. He's a good man, and I know he'll treat you right."

The three older women at the table, Mrs. Oliva Andrews, Mrs. Cecilia Bridges, and Mrs. Ethel Craskin, members of the "hit and run squad" and regulars at the book club, nodded in agreement. "It's so wonderful to see young love blossom like this," Mrs. Craskin said with a smile.

"I just can't believe it," Courtney said with a shy smile. "I never thought I'd find someone like Justin, someone who accepts me for who I am and supports my dreams. He is determined to help me focus on my art, and I couldn't be more grateful."

Her friends all nodded, grinning. "And we can tell he's smitten with you, too," Nevaeh said with a laugh.

The conversation at the book club was engaging as the women discussed the latest developments in their own love lives and the romances of others in Sweetgum. Mrs. Zhang, Rochelle, and the three older women shared their experiences of being married and offered advice to their single friends. Brandi gushed about her relationship with Chris and the rest of the group teased her good-naturedly about marriage and settling down.

Despite the lighthearted atmosphere, Courtney couldn't shake her nerves. She knew she had to leave soon to get ready for her date with Justin, and the excitement and fear of the unknown were starting to get the best of her. As the conversation shifted to the book of the week, *A Duke, A Doily, and A Dilemma*, Courtney found herself only half-listening. Her thoughts were preoccupied with what tonight would bring, imagining all sorts of possibilities.

"Earth to Courtney!" Nevaeh said with a laugh, snapping her out of her thoughts. "Distracted about tonight?"

Courtney's face heated, "Yes, I'm a little nervous about my date later," she admitted.

"How? It's with Justin, and he's so casual and nice" Joanne nodded, her eyes wide with excitement. "I can't believe you two are finally going on a date, though. It's a bit exciting, but no reason to be nervous. We all know he has fallen for you hard."

"I know he has, and it's been a long time coming," Courtney said with a smile. "I'm really looking forward to it, but I can't shake the nerves."

"We all are looking forward to it for you," Brandi said with a giggle. "You two are the talk of the town, you know."

"I guess we are," Courtney said, feeling a warm feeling in her chest.

The rest of the book club offered their well-wishes and encouragement, and before she knew it, it was time for Courtney to leave. And as she thought about her date with Justin, she realized that she was ready for whatever the future might hold. She just had to get over these first-date jitters.

"Okay, everyone, I've got to head out," Courtney announced, gathering her things and putting on her coat.

"Going to get ready for your big date, huh?" Rochelle teased with a smile.

"Yeah, I can't believe it's finally happening," Courtney said, her nerves showing in her voice.

"Don't be nervous, Courtney," Mrs. Zhang added. "Justin is a wonderful man. You two will have a great time."

"Thanks, Mrs. Zhang," Courtney said, smiling.

"I'll walk you out," Joanne offered, linking arms with her friend.

Once outside, Joanne turned to Courtney. "What's going on? You're shaking."

"I don't know," Courtney admitted. "I'm just so nervous. What if the date is terrible?"

"Oh, stop it," Joanne said, giving her a hug. "You two have been talking and flirting for months. It's going to be great. Just be yourself and have fun."

"Thanks, Joanne," Courtney said, feeling a little better. "I just like him so much. I want everything to be perfect."

"It will be," Joanne assured her. "Now, go get ready and have a fantastic time. I want all the details tomorrow."

"Details will be given," Courtney assured, hugging her again.

Joanne smiled at her friend. "Well, call us regardless of what happens tonight, okay? We want to hear all the juicy details."

"Ha! There probably won't be any juicy details," Courtney laughed, trying to hide her nervousness. "I mean, Justin is still cautious because of his ex-wife and wants to take things slow."

"Oh, I get it. He wants to make sure he's not jumping into anything too quickly. That's smart, Court," Joanne said, patting her arm comfortingly.

"Yeah, but what if tonight doesn't go well?" Courtney said, biting her lip.

"Girl, don't worry about it. You two have been getting along great, and the chemistry between you two is off the charts. Just be yourself and enjoy the night," Joanne said, smiling at her friend.

Courtney took a deep breath and smiled. "You're right. I'm just going to relax and have a good time. Thanks, Joanne."

"No problem, Court. Have fun tonight. And remember, we want all the details tomorrow!" Joanne called out as Courtney walked to her car, feeling a little more at ease.

As she drove home, Courtney felt giddy with excitement. All the time she and Justin had spent together over the past few months, getting to know each other and learning about each other's interests, had only served to deepen her feelings for him.

She felt confident that tonight would be a great start to something special, but she also knew that she needed to take things slow and not get ahead of herself. She was ready for whatever the night had in store and was looking forward to seeing where things would go between them.

As Courtney pulled into her driveway, her heart was racing. She was so nervous but also incredibly excited. As she walked through the door of her home, she could feel her nerves start to dissipate. She made her way up to her room and started getting ready. She was determined to make a great impression.

First, she did her hair and makeup. She went for a natural but glowing look, using the flat iron to loosen her curls, causing them to wave slightly. She wanted to look her best for Justin. She then checked her texts and saw one from Justin telling her he was excited and that he'd be exactly on time. She replied with a meme and an emoji and continued getting dressed.

She settled on a little black dress that fit her perfectly with a gently metallic and subtle bronze and copper design lining the collar. She paired it with matching jewelry, her favorite necklace, and some bracelets. She put a simple clip in her hair to hold it back from her face. She then inspected herself in the mirror and was pleased with what she saw.

As she was putting on the final touches, she saw Justin arrive through her window. Her heart raced with excitement. She accidentally put on a bit too much perfume and made her way to the front door. As she opened the door, she was greeted by Justin's handsome smile.

"You look beautiful," Justin said, his eyes lighting up as he took in Courtney's appearance.

"Thank you," Courtney replied softly. She was wearing her favorite dress and she felt confident and beautiful. He was wearing some nice jeans and a black t-shirt underneath a simple button-up vest, his light jacket pulling the look together quite nicely.

They made their way to the car, chatting and laughing as they went. Courtney was so thankful for Justin's presence. She felt like she could be herself around him, and that was a feeling she cherished. As they drove, they chatted about their day and the book club meeting.

"I'm really looking forward to this date," Justin said, taking Courtney's hand in his. "I've been looking forward to it since before we even agreed to it."

Courtney smiled, feeling a warmth spread through her chest. She was so thankful for Justin and for this moment. She was nervous about the date, but she was determined to enjoy every moment of it.

They arrived at the restaurant at the edge of town, and Courtney was impressed by the ambiance. It was a romantic candlelit Italian restaurant, and she couldn't wait to try the food. As Courtney and Justin arrived at the restaurant, they were greeted by the warm hostess. The soft lighting set a romantic mood, and the sounds of Italian opera music filled the air. They were seated at a quaint little table for two near the fireplace, with a beautiful red rose in a vase as the centerpiece.

"This place is beautiful," Courtney said, admiring the elegance of the restaurant. "I knew this place was here in Sweetgum, but I've never been."

"I'm glad you like it," Justin replied, smiling at her. "I wanted to take you somewhere special."

The menu was extensive, with many Italian delicacies to choose from. Courtney decided to go with the linguine alla carbonara, while Justin ordered the classic spaghetti Bolognese. As they ordered their meals, they continued to chat and laugh. Courtney was having the time of her life, and she couldn't wait to see where this relationship would go.

As they sipped their wine and waited for their food, they continued their light-hearted and romantic conversation. However, as they chatted and laughed, Justin accidentally knocked over his glass of red wine. Courtney giggled as Justin tried to wipe it up, but the wine only seemed to spread. Their server quickly cleaned the mess.

"I'm so sorry," Justin said, looking embarrassed once they were alone.

"Don't worry about it," Courtney replied, smiling jokingly. "It just adds to the ambiance."

When their food arrived, they were both in awe of the presentation. The dishes were beautifully arranged and the aromas wafting from the plates were tantalizing. As they took their first bites, they both moaned in delight at the delicious flavors.

Throughout the meal, Justin attempted to impress Courtney by speaking a little bit of Italian. Unfortunately, his pronunciation was terrible, and Courtney giggled at his efforts.

"Parli Italiano?" Justin said, trying to sound suave.

"Si, un po," Courtney replied, trying to hold back her laughter.

Despite the minor mishap and Justin's linguistic struggles, the night was filled with love, laughter, and delicious food. The couple sat in the restaurant for a while longer, chatting and laughing over the rest of their wine. Courtney couldn't remember the last time she felt so comfortable and happy with someone. As they finished their drinks, they decided to go for a walk in the park.

As they strolled through the park, they encountered some locals, including Everly, the librarian. She greeted them with a warm smile, and they chatted briefly before moving on. The sun was beginning to set, and the park was starting to empty out.

Finally, they found a quiet bench near a small pond. They sat down and took in the peaceful surroundings. As they sat there, Justin put his arm around Courtney and pulled her close. They kissed, and Courtney felt like she was in a fairy tale. It was so romantic, and she couldn't believe this was really happening to her.

As they continued to kiss, they were interrupted by a loud barking. They both looked around, and a small corgi with a blue collar and tag was running toward them. Justin was smitten and got down on one knee to pet the dog. It was the cutest thing Courtney had ever seen.

Just then, they heard someone calling out for a dog in the park. They looked up and saw a teenage girl waving at them, looking worried. "Louie!" she called. "Come back here!"

Courtney and Justin called the dog over, and the girl ran

over to them. "Thank you so much," she said, catching her breath. "He got away from me and I was so worried."

The girl explained that Louie was a rescue and had only been with her for a few months. Justin and Courtney could tell she loved the dog very much and they chatted with her for a few minutes before saying goodbye.

As they walked away from the pond and towards the park exit, Courtney looked at Justin and smiled. This had been the perfect evening. It was light-hearted, romantic, and full of laughter.

"I don't want the night to end," Justin admitted softly. "I… would it be too forward to invite you back to my place? Above the shop?"

"I've never been upstairs there," she chuckled, holding him close. "I would like to see your place."

"Really? Cause I don't want you to think I'm just trying to get you to come back to my place for something you're not ready for…."

"No, I get it," she laughed, cheeks heating. "We can go slow and just enjoy one another's company for a bit longer. I'd really like that."

"Yeah?" he questioned, holding her close. "My place is pretty nice, and I have a great view from the terrace."

"There's a terrace?"

"There is!" he chuckled. "I've got a terrace, some wine, and some snacks. How does that sound?"

"Entirely too good…"

As they walk to the watch shop, they held hands and chatted about how much fun they had at the restaurant and the park. Courtney smiled; she was having such a great time with Justin. They arrived at the watch shop and Justin lead her up the stairs to the apartment above the shop. The door opened to a large living room with big windows and a stunning view of

Sweetgum Meadows. What was more beautiful was his terrace outside the glass doors.

"Wow, this is beautiful," Courtney exclaimed as she walked over to the window.

"I'm glad you like it," Justin said with a shy smile. "I wanted to show you my favorite view in Sweetgum."

They sat on the couch on his terrace together, taking in the view and talking about the different places they had been to in the state park. Justin shared stories about hiking trips he had taken, and Courtney told him about her love for nature walks and the inspiration it provided for her art.

"Wow," she breathed, "This view really is amazing."

Justin smiled, "I'm glad you like it, truly."

He pulled her closer on the couch, where they sat side by side, admiring the view. The apartment was cozy and inviting, with soft lighting and a few well-placed candles. They talked about their day and shared more about their interests and their lives. The conversation flowed easily, and they felt as though they'd known each other for years.

Courtney leaned her head against Justin's shoulder, feeling completely at ease in his company. "You know, I never imagined that I'd end up on a first date in such a beautiful apartment," she said with a soft chuckle.

Justin grinned, "Well, I like to impress," he said playfully, brushing a strand of hair out of her face.

Courtney laughed, "You definitely succeeded."

They continued to talk and laugh, their conversation taking them from their favorite movies to their shared love of art. As the night wore on and the wine flowed, the mood between them became more playful and flirty.

Justin leaned in close to Courtney, his voice low, "I have to admit, I've been thinking about this moment all night."

Courtney felt a flutter in her stomach at his words. "Oh

really? And what moment is that?" she asked, her voice laced with amusement.

Justin's eyes flickered to her lips, "The moment I finally get to kiss you," he said with a hint of a smirk.

Courtney's heart raced at his words, and she found herself leaning in towards him as their lips met in a sweet and gentle kiss.

Courtney felt her heart race as Justin leaned in, his hand moving to her waist. She met his gaze, her eyes filled with a mix of nervousness and excitement. Justin's touch was electric, and she felt a spark of attraction between them.

Justin's eyes never left hers as he leaned in and pressed his lips to hers. Courtney melted into the kiss, feeling her body respond to his touch. Their lips moved in perfect harmony, and she felt a warmth spreading through her body.

As they pulled away, Justin looked at her with a smile. "Wow," he said, "I've been wanting to do that all night."

Courtney smiled back, her cheeks flushed with excitement. "Me, too," she whispered.

They leaned in for another kiss, this time more urgent and passionate. Courtney wrapped her arms around Justin's neck, deepening the kiss. She felt his hands move to her waist, pulling her closer to him.

As they finally pulled away, they were both breathing heavily, their eyes locked in a silent conversation as it seemed he struggled to keep his passions in check. She wouldn't force him; she know he wanted to take things slow. Courtney knew at that moment that she wanted to spend every moment with Justin.

They sat in comfortable silence for a few moments, lost in their thoughts and the beauty of the view. The stars shone brightly in the sky, and the sound of crickets filled the air.

As the night wore on, they continued to talk and kiss, reveling in the connection they had found. They knew that they had something special, and they didn't want to let it go. It was almost midnight by the time they had stopped kissing, the cool night air cooling them both.

"I should go," Courtney whispered, hoping he'd invite her to stay.

"Let me make sure you get home," he said, standing.

"It's safe," she giggled, motioning to the town around them from the terrace. "But I appreciate that."

"At least let me walk you down the block," he whispered, kissing her neck.

"Alright," she sighed, kissing his lips gently before pulling away.

Courtney arrived back at her home twenty minutes later, feeling on top of the world. She smiled as she thought about the evening they had just shared. She immediately text Joanne, who she knew was still awake, eager to share the details of her date with her best friends.

As she locked her front door, her phone rang, and she answered to hear Joanne's voice on the other end. Brandi and Nevaeh were also on the call, making it a full-blown group chat. Courtney quickly got undressed and changed into her pajamas as she talked to her friends about the amazing night she had just had.

"So, how was the date?" Joanne asked, excitement evident in her voice.

"It was amazing," Courtney replied, a huge smile spreading across her face. "We went to this Italian restaurant and the food was to die for. And then we went for a walk in the park and just talked and laughed and it was so romantic."

Her friends were eager to hear more, asking her questions and making comments about how sweet Justin seemed. They also discussed what they thought might happen next and what they thought about Justin as a potential partner for Courtney.

"I can tell he really likes you," Brandi said, "he sounds so sweet and romantic."

"I know," Courtney replied, still beaming, "I really like him too."

The conversation continued for a while longer, with the girls chatting and laughing.

As Courtney talked with her friends about her date with Justin, she could hear the excitement in their voices. Joanne, Brandi, and Nevaeh were all curious about why she hadn't stayed the night with Justin after their date. Courtney explained to them that she and Justin wanted things to be natural and that they didn't want to rush into anything too quickly.

"I just think it's important to take things slow, you know?" Courtney said, settling back into her bed. "We both have been through a lot in our past relationships, and we don't want to repeat those mistakes."

Her friends nodded in agreement and asked about the next date. Courtney beamed as she told them about their upcoming date, which was in two nights. She was excited to see Justin again and to spend more time with him.

"And the best part is, I get to see him tomorrow at the watch shop!" she exclaimed. "I can't wait."

Brandi and Nevaeh squealed with excitement while Joanne chuckled. "Well, we can't wait to hear all about it, Court. Have a great time on your next date."

Courtney thanked her friends for their support and for always being there for her. As they finally said their goodbyes and hung up, Courtney climbed into bed with a smile on her face, feeling content and happy. She couldn't wait to see what the future held for her and Justin and was grateful for the amazing night they had just shared.

CHAPTER TWENTY

Soft yellow string lights wrapped the wooden railings. They'd stepped off leveled ground to climb the staircase. The more they advanced, the more the steps seemed to bend at their weight. Justin knew they'd never give in, though. They were too sturdy. According to Sean, the creaks had been sounding since he was young. Sean's last visit to these trails was a while back, but he'd assured Justin that crossing the bridge to the lake would be romantic. So far, Justin had to agree. With his specially requested lights up for their date and the full moon glowing between tree branches, he could see what his friend had meant. *Thanks for the idea, Sean,* he'd say this in person later.

"Did you really ask them to do this for us?" Courtney asked as they followed the bridge. Despite the time of year, fallen leaves seemed to cover the floor. Justin assumed they'd flown off when the wind blew. Now and then, it rustled the branches and sent twigs to their clothes. "These decorations are so beautiful," she hugged their blanket close to her chest, seeming content to carry it.

Justin listened to the stream as it ran. He watched the water flow under their feet through slits in the wood. "Ah well, I just wanted to make sure that we saw where we were going on our way to the lake," he noted her admiration for their surroundings and patted himself on the back. She wore an easy smile on her glossy lips, bending her neck to stare at the trees.

"That's sweet. I can assure you that everything is clear right now. Clear and beautiful too. Thank you," she bumped her hip against the basket when he whispered a 'you're welcome'. "Still don't think it's too heavy? We can switch who holds what you know. I wouldn't want your arms getting tired," she moved her folded blanket so it fit beneath her arm. "Even if they are strong."

Justin appreciated the compliment. He flexed his bicep and then raised the basket. "I'm good. I don't want you tiring yourself out before we get there," he stopped at the end of the bridge and insisted that she take the first step down.

"Thank you," Courtney led the way until stopping near a boulder under a tree. "Don't have much more to go now." she faced the lake which lay beyond the path ahead. The moonlight shone above it and sparkled on the water. "This is going to be so much fun."

Justin caught up to her and whistled at the view. They'd have to walk down a grassy incline to get there. "Well, I hope it is. Oh, and I also hope that you like my special sauce." She'd laughed when he brought it up before. Ensuring her relaxation and happiness had become important to him. She was… great. So different from the last woman he'd fallen for. But he wasn't here to make comparisons.

"Oh, I *know* I will. What did you say was in it again?" Courtney made room for him beside her while strolling ahead.

Justin gladly took the cue. "It's a secret," he chirped. "But we'll see if you can guess once you've had a bite of the chicken sandwich."

"Okay. Adding a bit of mystery to this. I like it," she folded her arms over the blanket. "And maybe if your taste buds are sharp, you can figure out what makes my Shephard's pie so creamy. Think you can handle that?" She leaned in on him with a sultry expression.

Justin liked this. He liked this a lot. "So, it's turning into some kind of taste bud contest now?" he got lost in her eyes of mischief, loving the way they reflected the light. Being alone on this trail gave him this surreal sense of solitude. Like he and Courtney had the earth to themselves. The hypnotic silence of the woods was heavenly and their voices, footsteps and casual conversation set the mood for tranquility.

"If you're up for the challenge," Courtney swayed innocently before humming a tune. "Oh, wait. Is it really not that heavy to you?" she gestured to the basket.

"What? This?" Justin loved her concern, but he really was okay. "Court, it's just sandwiches, pies, and drinks in here. We haven't even been walking that long. I'm okay. Really," he raised it like a weight in the gym. "I've lifted pillows heavier than this thing," he might as well show off while they were on the topic.

Courtney drew out a 'really' then jogged ahead of him. She walked backward with their blanket to her chest. "Does that mean you can hold your own in a race to the lake right now?" She seemed shy about asking, shifting her eyeballs from his face to the ground.

What a delightful surprise! Playfulness meant comfort. She'd been a little tense on their last date from what he recalled, but tonight she was loose as a string. Had the fancy restaurant been intimidating? They'd had a good time in the end so her tension must have stemmed from the pressure of a first date. He'd hidden it well, but Justin had been nervous too. "Of course. My legs are longer. I think I'd win, no problem."

She showed her doubt in an arched left eyebrow. "Is that so? Well… let's see!" she dashed off like an excited little kid.

"Hey!" Justin raced after her with the basket jerking. "You

cheat!" he caught up in seconds, then passed her with ease. "See what I mean? Long legs!" he hollered over his shoulder.

Courtney ran faster but struggled to reach him. She eventually stopped to catch her breath.

Justin slowed down before changing course, running to her instead of away. "You okay?" he said while panting. "I hope nothing spilled in here," he gently shook their basket.

Courtney held both knees with her head pointing downward. "I'm sure everything's okay. I just needed to take the lead real quick!" She left him in the dust with her speed.

Justin couldn't believe she tricked him a second time. "Oh, Courtney," he wondered what summoned this friskiness. "Even with a second head start, I'll win," he would give chase, but it was in their food's best interest that he didn't. "Run like the wind, Court!" he blew out a laugh as he sped-walked behind her.

They got to the lake at long last. He'd helped her with spreading their blanket over the grassy hillside before setting down the basket. She'd taken a seat in the middle of the blanket and patted beside her to indicate his place, crossing her legs after doing so.

Justin settled to her left like she wanted and dragged the basket to his lap. "Let's see if anything's spilled in here." He flipped open the lid and pulled out their drinks. "These held up pretty well, didn't they?" He put down the bottled orange juice, then removed a bowl of strawberries.

Courtney retrieved his wrapped sandwiches while he steadied the bowl. Next, she dipped her hand in for her container of pie. "The stars are amazing tonight," she commented.

Justin flashed them a look and agreed. "Feels like everything's working with us, doesn't it?" He set aside their basket when all the food was out. "That means we should make the best of this. Because we don't know when we'll get another perfect evening like this one." He took both her hands to hold between his.

"You're right," she seemed mesmerized by him, and he truly felt the same but with her. It elated him to know that she shared his excitement about this. He wasn't in love alone like he'd been in the past. They were about to have a picnic that they'd planned together and would both have fun with. What more could he ask for?

TWENTY MINUTES LATER, caught him guessing. Courtney had figured out the elements of his sauce pretty quickly, but her Shephard's pie posed a challenge to him. "Uh, is it… mayonnaise? It's so good I can't get enough of it," he used his plastic spoon to scoop up some more. The plastic wrapping of their sandwiches had been disposed of in the nearby trash can. Neither he nor Courtney intended on sullying the beautiful trails with their debris. A few rangers had walked by to remind them of nearby bins.

"Nope," Courtney took a sip of her juice. They'd poured them into disposable cups. "I couldn't heat it up in the microwave with mayonnaise in it, could I? Remember I said I'd heated it?" she played with the collar of her electric blue blouse. It was hidden under her denim jacket. Though summer nights tended to be warm, cool winds weren't unheard of. Justin wore a jacket of his own for that reason. It covered his black polo.

"Oh yeah, yeah," he ate the rest and praised her culinary skills. "I don't know what you put in that, but it's good." He wiped his mouth with a napkin while she clapped in hysterics. "What?"

Courtney dusted something away from his face, then sat closer. "I just find it endearing how you gave up but kept eating anyway. Not that I'd expected you to throw it out because you couldn't guess, but it's just the combination of things." She had a hand on his lap.

Justin melted under her touch. Her palm felt warm, and her smile soothed him. He put his own hand on top of hers and traced a thumb over her knuckles. "You know, while I've grown to trust you and learn how honest you are on top of being caring… there's still this annoying voice in the back of my head that says this is all fake and that what happened last time will happen with you," he heard distant discussions from rangers on the trails. The leaves separated when threads of breeze traveled through them. Near the lake, trees were absent, but they stood in abundance on the hill above it.

Courtney fit her hand in his and held on tightly. "It's normal to have doubts for a while after something like that, but you just need to keep trusting me, okay? I'll never hurt you the way she did. I'm not her. I'm me, and I think by now you should know what I'm like," she brushed a hand up his arm.

He breathed out as goosebumps covered his skin, a rush traveling through him. "I know. Sorry, Courtney. You've heard more than enough about this, yet here I am bringing it up again. I never want to push you away—"

"I'm not going anywhere," she whispered the words on his cheek. "Justin, look at me."

He did, catching the intensity of her eyes. Love, hope, and worry all mashed together to give them that impression. "I'm looking… and I like what I see," he confessed without thought. "Do you like what you see in me? Be honest," he held on tightly, probably cutting off circulation in her fingers. "I'm sorry to down the mood, but it's just nagging."

"No one deserves to be cheated on or made to feel unworthy, like what happened to you. I understand why it keeps bothering you, so don't apologize," she tugged their hands to her lap. "I haven't gone through what you have, but a few horrible partners of mine in the past have done some pretty awful things. Not to the same degree since we weren't married, but I remember how it made me feel," she leaned away.

This sparked his interest and also annoyed him. "What? Did someone cheat on you? Perfect Courtney?" he cracked his neck. "Where is he?"

Courtney pushed him lightly in a joking manner. "Nothing like what you've been through. A couple of guys have treated me badly in the past. Like this guy from high school who I'd dated for about a month until my friends caught him making out with someone under the bleachers...." She untangled her hand from his to hold up a finger.

Justin put down a palm behind him for support. "Really? Why would he do that? Was he some kind of player or a complete idiot? I guess they're interchangeable," he stroked his chin while she giggled.

"I don't know what his deal was, but at that age, it *hurt* to know that he'd done that. I cried for weeks." Courtney pounded her fist on her knee for emphasis. "*Ugly* cried for weeks, actually. You wouldn't have wanted to see me." she plucked a stray string from his pocket.

"I'd want to see you any way that you are as long as you're yourself," Justin admitted, examining his pocket. "How long did it take you to date again after that?" he commended himself for flustering her with that last compliment.

Courtney seemed to struggle with gathering her wits. "Uhhh..." she stumbled. "Oh, I dated like a month after it happened. The other guy was okay, but I got cheated on again around college, so that wasn't fun at all." She lifted her cup and finished her drink. "Yeah, it's just so messed up, but we've both gone over this, right?" she stared at the lake.

He followed her, listening to its subtle motions against the dock. At that point, he took her hand again, loving how she naturally intertwined their fingers. "Yeah, we have." he looked at the silver bracelet she wore on her wrist. "Promise me we'll always be honest with each other and that we'll…."

"Be there for one another?" Courtney suggested.

"Yeah," Justin faced her again, their noses bumping. He slightly pulled away to make room. "That we'll not only support each other but build each other up. Never tear each other down."

Courtney gave firm nods to each of these statements. "I promise. I promise," she rested her forehead against his, shutting her eyes. "I promise, Justin Clark. I don't want to hurt you or break you down. I'm glad I could be the one to help heal you. I want to keep it that way. To add on to what's already been restored," she said it like a prayer, enchanting him with each spoken word.

Justin's eyes misted. "And I want to repay you for all you've done to help me by doing the same. I'll keep you on your feet and help you to walk when you need it. I'll cheer you on whenever you try something new and need me there. I want to be there for you. I want you to have a friend in me and to be someone you can confide in just like I confided in you. I want to be that for you. I promise to be that for you," he cupped her face with both hands.

Courtney opened her eyes, and they connected with his.

Gently, he positioned his face so it fit against hers and their lips made contact. Just like their first, they started off softly before navigating into fiery make-out territory. From there, they accepted and received each other with passion.

Justin's back hit the mat when Courtney straddled his waist. With her body hovering over him, her lips devoured his senselessly. He slipped his hand under her top, then stopped himself. "Wait."

Courtney kissed him one last time before disconnecting. "Everything alright?" she suddenly rolled away and sat upright, hand over her mouth and eyes surveying the lake.

Justin sat up, too, sharing her look of disbelief. Luckily, apart from the wandering rangers, not a soul was in sight. He turned to Courtney, and they both snorted with laughter. "How crazy was that? And out in the open, too."

"We're insane." Courtney held her wrist to her mouth, then batted her lashes.

Justin pressed his top row of teeth against his bottom lip. He began packing the rest of their stuff, then showed Courtney his best look of seduction. "Want to come over to my place for drinks?" his heart pounded like a sledgehammer as the words left his mouth. Every hair on his body stood up, and vicious flames heated his system. As the exhilaration increased, he wondered if she felt it too. *I know she does.* She'd shown him through their kiss.

Courtney smiled and slid a hand over her hair. "I'd love that."

CHAPTER TWENTY-ONE

$\mathcal{D}$aybreak crept between her eyelids and forced them to open.

Courtney was greeted by Justin's sleeping form, his chest rising delicately with every breath he took. He seemed dead to the world from this angle. If it weren't for his breathing, she'd mistake him for a corpse. He made no other movements as he lay; no thrashing or turning or shifting in the slightest. His serenity was tempting. She toyed with the idea of going back to sleep but had chores awaiting her at home.

So, she rose out of bed and peeled his white sheets from her body before crawling to the edge and quietly climbing out. With arms on her chest, Courtney searched the carpeted floors for her clothes. Justin's black polo was spotted near the dresser, but her top and jeans were nowhere in sight. While standing exposed, she contemplated her next decision.

It fit like a dress but was comfy. His heavenly musk fused with his brand name cologne had her basking in the scent of his fabric. Courtney concluded that this satisfied her and left for the kitchen.

SHE'D SAID her goodbyes after breakfast.

While Justin apologized infinitely for waking so late, Courtney had insisted it wasn't an issue. Making him breakfast was the least she could do after their amazing night together. Over their food, their conversation flowed naturally, with Justin sneaking in compliments here and there. They ranged from how effortlessly gorgeous he found her to praising her work on their eggs. Courtney appreciated every one of them, pleased to be the source of his happiness. He'd suffered for too long by himself, tormented by the trauma of his failed marriage. There'd never been an instance in her life where she'd contributed to someone's healing. It boosted her sense of self.

Justin had located her clothing for her so that she could change before leaving. He thanked her countlessly for being who she was and bringing him joy. And, of course, she'd thanked him for presenting her his all the night before. Recalling it sent a rush up her back. She wished for more close encounters and wholesome mornings with him.

The sky seemed brighter as she strolled down the sidewalk. Justin had planned on driving her home since he'd picked her up for their date, but Courtney preferred to walk. She needed the solitude to reflect on what happened and its incredible effects. Was she allowed this much contentment? She was beginning to notice beauty in places she'd never expected. Like her eyes had been opened for the first time since birth. Had she been reborn? Why were the lawns of her neighborhood so green and why was the sunlight so radiant against this parked convertible? She admired the way it fit in the garage of the house on her left. An older man used a hose to sprinkle his flowers. They sat in pots along his front porch. On her way down the path, she offered him an exuberant hello, finding it difficult to contain her own joy.

The man's face lit up with surprise. He showed her a smile and waved, asking how she felt.

"It's a lovely morning," Courtney told him. They shared a short laugh before she continued on. She whipped out her phone, inhaling the air of the crisp new day. "This might all be in my head," she said to herself, finding stray weeds peeping from cracks in the sidewalk. How wonderful was it that nature always found a way to rear its head? She did all she could to resist greeting the weed too. The hilarity of this struck her and she had to shake her head.

> Girls. We need to meet for coffee at ten. Got a lot to share.

She hit send on this message and awaited their replies. This chat belonged to her and her friends. There was never a dull moment with them. Almost every day, either Nevaeh or Joanne would send something crazy to spur ongoing discussions that sometimes lasted days. Courtney would always look forward to their whacky conversations, but of late, she'd been absent. Now and then, she'd scroll to catch up, but never added her input. Her mind had taken an interest in other things recently. Knowing her friends, though, they'd be understanding. They were aware of what kept her.

Without a second to spare, her friends sent texts to confirm they'd be present. Joanne teased her and her playful jeers invited the others to comment as well, mentioning Justin as the reason she'd 'abandoned' them. They hit the nail on the head with that one. Justin was to blame for her ghosting tendencies.

Courtney giggled at their light-hearted messages and texted that she'd fill them in when they met.

Her reflection seemed to gleam as she pulled on her jacket. She'd just changed out of her clothes from last night. Even the smallest of details ran amuck through her brain. The thread she'd pulled from Justin's clothes while they ate and how he'd plucked a leaf from her hair on their walk to the lake. She couldn't live it down. Everything replayed like a movie. Had she really lived that last night? What satisfied her the most was how he'd handled her after. The fact that a man like Justin existed all this time was mind-boggling. Where had he been all her life? Every box was ticked with Justin and she was beginning to fear that deeper feelings were manifesting. Was it too soon? *Three months.* Others fell hard in one second. She hadn't lost it, right?

Courtney rubbed her hands down her cheeks while exhaling. While she was getting ready, she smiled and relive the night before. Because of that, the process had been prolonged with her frequent disconnections. Ten a.m. would soon be upon her and she'd hate to keep her girls waiting. Their advice was necessary here, as she could not trust herself. She felt like a character put under a love spell, so blindly infatuated she barely thought coherently.

"Okay. Enough of this. I need to go," she said to her reflection, then rushed to her bed. After putting on her handbag, she went to the door and swung it wide open, hoping she'd make it to Joanne's in time.

⁂

The sound of Nevaeh's signature cackle brought glee to her overflowing heart.

"Another busy morning, Jo?" Courtney asked, inhaling the splendid aroma of bagels and coffee beans. The line at the desk was six customers long, and the tables and chairs held many. Every face she caught sight of held delight. Laughter, talking, and eating were the surrounding noises. She couldn't picture a better setting.

Joanne playfully smacked Nevaeh to quiet her down. She grabbed hold of a salt shaker when Courtney sat in front of them. "Oh yeah. You know Saturdays. They're like Friday nights but with the sun outside. The people love coming in at this hour, but by afternoon it'll be a ghost town in here," she deflected a soft hit from the playful Nevaeh. Joanne eventually held her shoulders to keep her still.

"Courtney, you look amazing." Brandi pulled Courtney close once she sat to her right. She rested an arm over Courtney's shoulders and nuzzled her cheek.

Courtney reveled in the affection, suddenly realizing how much she'd missed them. Not long had passed since they last interacted, but there'd once been a time when they met every day. *Back in high school,* she sighed as a wave of nostalgia threatened to consume her. "Thanks, Brands, but I'm not wearing anything different." A plate of scones was at the center of their table. She took one and bit, loving the jam that stuck to her teeth. "Mm, are these new to the menu?"

"No, actually. They're just not all that popular. Guess it's because we don't live in England. Don't they eat scones over there?" Joanne pondered briefly, then shrugged. "Anyway, what's this meeting all about, Court?"

Courtney twirled her hair in innocence, listening as Nevaeh asked similar questions, a few light-hearted jokes sprinkled in. As her friends went on, she hurried to defend herself. "Guys, you know I've been busy with not only work but what's been going on with me and Justin."

"Aww," Brandi put her elbows on the table while using her hand to squish her own cheeks. "I don't know, but there's just something so adorable about sharing a business with your boyfriend," she blew kisses for Courtney.

"Of course. It is *so* cute, but did you guys seal the deal?"

Nevaeh stopped joking around to ask. She shook herself like a cell phone on vibrate. Clearly, Courtney's love life was interesting in her eyes. "I know you've been on what? One date? But is that enough?" she played with her twist out by tugging a strand. It immediately recoiled when she released it.

Joanne weighed in before Courtney could answer. "It's more than enough if they also work together. It means they spend every winking moment of the day with each other. They're practically married. Isn't that right, Courtney?" she lifted a scone and bit hungrily, covering her mouth with her palm when she chewed.

"Not exactly. I mean, technically, since we spend so much time together, it should automatically mean that we were already dating, right?" Courtney nibbled her own scone and chewed carefully, not quite sure of the taste yet. *Not bad.* She went in for a full bite.

"I think so. But just to be clear, you should ask him soon. Ask if he's your boyfriend and you're his girlfriend. Middle school style," Brandi pressed her shoulder on Courtney while wriggling her eyebrows. A napkin full of crumbs sat on the table before her, leading Courtney to wonder what she'd eaten.

"Middle school," these girls were too adorable. "Yeah, I think it's just a given now that we're together. I mean..." Courtney's skin turned to fire at vivid memories. Their time in his room, their kiss at the park, that silly race she'd started. Their guessing game... she longed for more and needed it urgently.

"Wait, wait, wait," Nevaeh gasped sharply, a slow grin emerging. "What's with that face? You mean what? Did something happen? Did we miss something?" she moved to the edge of her seat and slammed her hands on the table, pushing her face forward in evident expectation. "Spit it out, Court. What happened?"

"She *means* they've been seeing each other for a while, so they must be together. Right?" Joanne was halfway through her scone. She licked jam off her lip and then sucked some off her thumb. Her wonderful nails had jam beneath them. Courtney saw this even from here. She sat directly across from Joanne while Brandi faced Nevaeh. They often chose this arrangement for their meetings.

Courtney folded her hands a few times. "No. Last night we actually did something... Special. As in, we got to know each other even better... at his apartment," the more she revealed, the more her friends reacted. They were quiet about it, but their enthusiasm resonated. While Joanne jumped in place with a hand fanning her neck, Nevaeh clapped silently, her teeth bared in delight. Meanwhile, Brandi's eyes seemed to bulge as she held the sides of her face. She eventually grabbed Courtney's wrist and leaned closer.

"You have to tell us everything," Brandi whispered.

Nevaeh shushed Brandi. "Courtney doesn't have to give details, though we'd *love* to hear them. Me. 'We' is me. I want to know," she raised her hand for emphasis.

"You two are going to make her stop talking. You know that she's shy when it comes to her feelings," Joanne shushed them and sat forward. "Honestly, Court, he seems so nice," she pouted and patted the area under her breast, touching her heart. "When you talk about him, it makes me wish I had that."

"Brandi can relate," Nevaeh's mouth was full of scones. She'd just taken one for herself. Three remained.

"You guys aren't letting her speak. I'm sure there's more she'd like to tell us. I mean, she called a meeting," Brandi's arm was around Courtney, her elation evident in her voice and expression. Show wore an infectious smile, causing Courtney's to grow in length.

"Honestly, I don't mind listening to you guys ramble. It's so funny when you share your opinions," Courtney admitted. She bit another piece of her pastry, jam getting on her lips. Brandi instinctively wiped it away, and she thanked her. "Yes, he was amazing to me and that paired with everything else about him just makes him perfect. He was always perfect, but we talked even more last night, and I just love his vulnerability. He's so open, and he wants us to be open with each other in our relationship. I couldn't agree more because, half the time, the reason modern love stories fail is a lack of communication. To find a man who knows the value in that is just... he's a gift. He keeps saying I saved him, but what if he saved me? I was so disillusioned until I met him." She savored every bit of her scone, noting her friends' attentiveness. Their faces held fondness. "I don't know, since the day I brought my watch to his shop, my life has had meaning," she heard their collective agreement. "It's been three months, but we've spent every day together. He's not just my partner, but a close friend. He's so easy to talk to and sensitive and adorable. I can't even sit here and act like I'm not head over heels for this man, guys." her eyes stung as tears visited them. "I love him."

To that, her friends turned to mush, a string of 'aww's leaving their mouths.

"You love him?" mouthed Nevaeh while dropping her scone.

"Are you sure, or is this the high talking? When someone treats you right, they tend to look flawless the day after. Not that I don't believe you. I just want to be sure. You're thinking clearly, right? Your face is so shiny, Courtney. Not shiny in a bad way, but it's like you're a star. You're radiating," Joanne blabbered hurriedly, alternating between sitting back and forward. "I'm sorry, this is just so sweet. *I'm* not thinking straight." she flung her hair off her shoulders, using the back of her palm to do so.

Brandi had positioned her arm around Courtney. "I know. But I think she's sure." she stroked Courtney's shoulder in a motherly way. "The shine your seeing is love. Court doesn't jump to conclusions that way."

Courtney gripped the front of her top near her belly. "I

don't, but it feels like I am. That's why I wanted you guys to share how you felt about this." even with Joanne's doubts laid out before her, her feelings didn't sway. "I don't know, it's… it's crazy. Do you think I'm crazy, Jo?"

Nevaeh rested a hand on Joanne's cheek, pushing her aside. "Don't listen to her. I think you know how you feel and that your feelings are valid. You two are perfect for each other. You have every right to be in love. It's not like he's some random man she suddenly bumped into. This is Justin. We all like him—ah!" she pulled back when Joanne bit her pinky. "Jo!"

Joanne snickered like a problem student. "I'm sorry, Nev," she kissed where she bit. "I wasn't trying to shut you down, Courtney. I was just checking, you know?"

"Yes, yes. I totally understand that." Courtney ate the last of her scone. "I think that this is really how I feel and that Justin is special. Yeah. Even if it hasn't been long," she touched the side of her neck with her palm.

"Oh, trust me. It's been more than enough time for love to develop. Some people fall in less than a day. In an hour even," Brandi held Courtney's knee under the table.

Customers went in and out as they sat there, but she hardly took heed. Right now, Courtney's focus was glued to her friends, their opinions and comments. "Yeah, that's what I was thinking. So, it's valid," she put her hand over Brandi's, and they shared a soft giggle.

"Okay, and?" Joanne prompted, snatching Courtney's attention.

Courtney looked over at her archly. "Okay, and what?" Joanne's lips were curled in a smirk as she batted her eyelashes smugly. Her attitude of mischief was pleasing to witness.

"You know that you love him, so what's the next step? Will you tell him? Wait it out? Propose?" Joanne snuck that last one in, but Courtney heard her.

"Propose?" Courtney quickly dismissed the suggestion. "No

way. We're not ready for that. Just because I'm in love with him doesn't mean he's in love with me. I mean, he might be, but I don't know. What if he needs more time? *We* need more time. We just started dating." she lifted another scone from the plate.

"She was just joking, Courtney," Nevaeh flicked Joanne on the arm. Joanne seemed content with the fright she'd spurred in Courtney.

Courtney waved her off. "You're never serious and it's hilarious." She rolled her eyes fondly. "Anyway, I just thought you guys should know, seeing that you're practically my sisters and everything," she set the scone on her napkin, her stomach finally satisfied.

"We *are* your sisters, and we are so happy for you. Love is a beautiful thing, Court. Everyone deserves to have it," Brandi expressed earnestly. She dusted some crumbs off her hands. "I think that from here, things will only get better for you and Justin."

"Oh yeah, definitely. You two just work," Nevaeh chimed in while raising her mug. "And can I just say that you being in love is the cutest thing? Guys I'm so happy for her," she whined like she'd been inconvenienced or bothered.

Courtney was touched, aware that Nevaeh only became this way when excessively happy. "Thank you. I appreciate your support," she blew kisses for Joanne, who'd blown kisses herself. As her friends continued their doting, her world grew even brighter. Every customer shone like jewels and the dinging cash register was a bell to her ear. *Thank you, Justin.*

CHAPTER TWENTY-TWO

losing hour was just five minutes away but Courtney was still busy with phone calls. It'd been this way all day thanks to their expanded overseas clientele. Since Courtney had joined him, they'd only grown in number, her charm and sense of negotiation being the reason.

From day one, Justin had known she was gifted, but she'd only proven her exceptionality as time drew on. She got to business, charmed prospects and worked with efficiency. Sometimes, Justin would stand aside to admire her. Just yesterday he'd been blessed to witness her incredible multi-tasking where she'd sealed a deal via phone call while preparing payment forms for a physical client. Justin loved spending his days close to Courtney and all the time they spent together had only worked to strengthen that. If they could breathe the same air for all eternity, he'd never complain again.

"I'm going to start closing up," he sauntered away from his office and moved past her desk. Before arriving at the door though, he walked back then rested his arms upon her glossy wooden furniture.

Courtney hung up on a call with an air of geniality. "Oh, hey

Justin. Did you say something?" she clicked her pen to sign some forms. Three folders were stacked to her left. On top of being a go-getter, she maintained tidiness at her workstation and did the same with Justin's. She'd arranged the files in his office alphabetically a few days ago, a project they'd tackled together.

Justin got lost in her eyes. Was it just him or had her levels of beauty recently increased? "I was just saying I would lock up. It's getting late. The sun's about to go down," his eyes wandered to the desk. "And we wouldn't want to wait too long before we leave. Doesn't the ice cream parlor close before eight?" he locked eyes with her again.

"Oh yeah," Courtney gasped but her stun dimmed gradually. "Wait, but there's an ice cream truck that drives around town. We can get our treats there if you want. Unless you really wanted to sit in that parlor. Around now a lot of parents take their kids over there," she slid a finger down his knuckle.

He shuddered in gratification, loving the skin contact. Before she could pull away, he held onto her hand and kissed it. "As long as I have ice cream with you, I'm happy, okay? If you know any nice spots we can eat there," he could not resist kissing her a second time.

Courtney lowered her face in glaring bashfulness. "Aww, well… okay," she tugged on his hand until it tapped her own lips. Then, she kissed it. "I know somewhere nice. Just give me some time to pack up."

"I'll help. I'm just going to flip the 'closed' sign real quick," Justin reluctantly released his hand from her hold then walked towards the door.

With a click of the lock, they were all set to head off. The sidewalks were teaming with people on their way home from work. Cars drove in twos down the street and lamp posts were just lighting up.

"The thing about ice cream trucks is that they move,"

Courtney mentioned with wind in her hair. She had an arm hooked around Justin's while searching the streets. "It's usually near the diner, so we can check there. If we don't find it, our best bet might be to order our ice cream from the parlor, then walk to my spot."

Justin steered her away from some joggers. He re-hooked his arm into hers before speaking. "I think that might be best. What flavor do you want? Are you ready to explore other options? Cookie dough won't always be around, Court," he slipped her twists past her shoulder when they flew in her face.

"Who says so?" Courtney bumped him with her hip. "They don't just delete ice cream flavors," she said knowingly. The setting sun seemed to capture her attention. "Especially those beloved by all. What kind of person doesn't like cookie dough?" she held his arm with her free hand.

Some onlookers saw this and whispered. They gave them room to walk as they pleased. One man whistled as he passed on their left, causing laughter to rise from them both. Were they causing a scene? Walking hooked-arm wasn't that captivating. People got excited over the smallest of gestures.

Justin cared little for this attention. Courtney's presence brought symphonies to his soul, so he'd keep her near so long as she agreed. "Fair point, but I think you'd love some other flavors if you took the time to try them. I'm not forcing you, but it's a suggestion," he found her response hilarious. She'd wrinkled her face to a cringe that accentuated her cute features. He liked the look of her turned-up nose. "A bad suggestion, right?"

Courtney smiled with her head on his arm. "Okay. How about you order for me when we get there," she raised her eyes to look at him, giving her face a puppy-esque flare.

Justin's heart soared, and he fought his will to kiss her. He'd already done so twice in an hour. Stealing another in the public street would be overkill, no matter how tempting. "I'd love to. And if you don't like what I get you, you can have mine."

COURTNEY STOPPED to greet her friend on their way back from the ice cream place. He'd bought her a scoop of bubblegum ice cream and pistachio for himself. To his pleasant surprise, she'd loved her first spoonful. Just like she'd predicted, little kids and their parents had packed up the shop when they'd visited. But this served as a bother to neither of them. In fact, they'd quite enjoyed the bubbly spirits eagerly selecting their flavors. Innocence was a gift and precious to witness.

"Okay we're heading to the gazebo so you take care," Courtney ended her embrace with her friend outside the coffee shop, then waved her goodbye.

He gave Joanne a wave when Courtney held his hand. From there, they continued their journey. "Oh, so this secret location is the gazebo down Main Street?" he swung their hands moderately.

"Mhm," she let go of him and held onto her spoon. After scooping up a portion she licked the pink cream. "It's easier to see the sunset from there," she set her spoon delicately in her mouth and slurped up the rest. After licking her lips, she stuck the utensil into the rest of her treat. "Although the sun's basically set by now. Look."

Justin noted the dying light of burned orange hue. "We still have time, we're almost there," he quickened his pace. "We'll just have to race. But as a team instead of against each other," he chucked his spoon into his nearly-melted scoop. The thick milky substance half-filled his cup. His fingers tingled against the cold Styrofoam exterior.

"Good idea, Justin Clark." Courtney took his hand once again. "Shall we?"

"We shall." Besides a few teens nearing Roasted Beans Coffee Spot, the sidewalk was their own. Justin counted from three, and they flew down together like gleeful children. A sense of newness tended to pervade him when with her.

At long last, they arrived at the gazebo with desserts half-eaten. They both put their elbows on its rich wooden railing and stood side by side, shoulders touching. The woodsy styling of the octagonal gazebo fit the aesthetic of a perfect outdoor recreational facility. Built-in seats along the bordering railings provided a resting place for those who required it, and the conical roof overhead completed its structure.

"There's always this short green twinkle right after the sun sets," said Courtney, engrossed in the view. The sun had already sunk beyond the roofs of town structures. Faint light was left in its wake, leaving the sky a darker blue and its clouds fading slightly.

"Really? I've never seen that." he found the sight of her face more riveting than the sunset. As she described her encounters with this phenomenon, he hung onto each word. Her stories compelled him no matter their contents. He loved listening to her and the melodic nature of her voice. It was unspoken between them what they'd become, but he'd actually arranged this small date as a means to discuss it. Time and time again, they'd agreed to communicate and that went for this too. Just to ensure they were on the same page. He'd labeled her his own but was he hers in her subconscious? The answer was clear but he needed to hear it.

"Courtney?" he said when she finished her story. A few cyclists zipped up Main Street when she faced him, her bright eyes wide with curiosity. "I know that we've fallen for each other and it's obvious that we have, but in the name of openness and honesty, I'm just going to go ahead and say how I feel. I'd appreciate if you expressed your true feelings too. That is, if you want to. I don't want to—,"

"I will. I really want to. Go ahead, Justin. I'm listening." she removed her elbows from the railing to stand tall. With her cup between her hands, she awaited his declaration, her eagerness displayed in the bounce of her shoulders.

He, too, straightened, so they stood face to face. Once concealing his cup behind him, he began. "Courtney, since we've met and gotten closer, you've been nothing but patient, kind, and understanding with me. I know it can be tough to handle my baggage but you've never complained since the day I revealed it," his eyes connected to hers which were already moist. "I didn't mean to make you cry—" he caught a tear that raced down her cheek

"No, no, it's not your fault. Sorry. This is just sweet. Continue, please. Ignore me. I'm a crybaby," she sniffled with a hand over her jaw.

Was it weird to find her beautiful with tears in her eyes? "No, you're perfect. Let it out. It's what I'm doing too but differently. Never suppress yourself for anyone okay?" he kissed her cheek then reached for her hand. "Listen to me," he inched closer for intimacy. "I'm saying what we already know because voicing this is important. Just so you're certain how I feel about you," his breath landed upon her trembling lips. The puff of her eyes endeared him.

"Okay," she breathed. It tickled his face.

"I love you, Courtney, and it didn't take long for me to realize that. It's not just about liking an attractive girl who wowed me with her capabilities anymore. I deeply adore you. I'm saying this because I want you to know," he rested his forehead against hers.

She grinned after sniffing. "I know. I *have* known. But I love that you said it. We need to talk to each other and I'm glad you keep stressing that," she reached for his elbow to squeeze in her grip, setting her cup on the railing. Her delicate hand rubbed him with a soothing motion.

He relished in the solace of her hold. "You have no idea how relieving it is to hear you say that," he blew a short laugh onto her face as she smiled beatifically. "And because I love you, I want to call you my girlfriend. My lover who rescued me. Is that okay, Courtney? Do you want to be mine?" he searched her eyes for signs of doubt. She'd closed them at first, but now they were open.

Courtney's composed nod lit fireworks in his heart. She moved her hand from his elbow to hand and grasped it carefully. He'd rested his cup beside hers a second ago. "Yes, Justin. I'd be more than happy to be your official girlfriend." She tackled him with a hug and tightened her arms with zeal.

"Woah!" he almost fell back at the sudden affection. He returned the favor by holding her, too, and secured her balance with his body. "Be careful, Court. I'd hate for you to fall here," he warned as she hopped against him. They were on level ground, but the floor was still hard. At least, he presumed that it was. The wooden composition would likely cushion a harsh collision, but the best course of action was to avoid one entirely. "What's with all the bouncing?"

She let go of him. "It's because of you. You've got me feeling like a kid, Justin. Like a kid out for ice cream," she jovially tapped his nose with her finger. "I should say how I feel now, right? Although you can guess."

"I mean, it's written in your reaction, but again, honesty and—"

"Openness. Right, right," Courtney cheerfully raised both her shoulders.

He lost in the battle of concealing his grin. It spread like a paint drop in water, lifting his ears and narrowing his eyes with happiness. "Take your time," he urged, circling his thumbs against her hands.

Courtney brought their hands to her chin. "Justin, I think I've loved you before we even went on our first date. I've wanted us to make things official for a while, so I'm glad we have. You're so sweet and thoughtful for doing it this way. This feels like a fairytale," her nose scrunched on the laugh she let free.

His ears perceived it as music, fluttering his heart and elevating his already good mood. "I know. It feels the same for me, too," he put his arms on her shoulders. "So, it's official," hearing her say it explicitly had completed him.

"Indeed, it is," she reached for his shoulders. "But it wouldn't hurt to seal things with a kiss. Unless you're shy," Town Square had grown active beyond Main Street. Dogs chased after frisbees and a yoga class had commenced.

Justin cared not for these potential spectators. "They're in their world and we're in ours," at those words he dipped her like a ballroom dancer then bent in for a kiss.

EPILOGUE

Courtney stood nervously in front of the clock display at Justin's shop. He had asked her to come by and try her hand at customizing a clock with her art. She was unsure of herself and her abilities, but Justin had always been supportive of her art and encouraged her to try new things.

"Okay, so you want me to just paint right onto the clock face?" she asked tentatively, eyeing the clock in front of her.

Justin nodded. "Exactly. Just let your creativity flow and see where it takes you."

Taking a deep breath, Courtney picked up a paintbrush and began to carefully apply her design onto the clock face. At first, she was hesitant and unsure, but as she continued to work, she began to feel a sense of excitement and possibility.

After hours of work, Courtney stepped back to admire her painted clock. To her surprise, it looked amazing. The colors were vibrant, and her design was unique and eye-catching.

As they put the clock on display, customers started to notice not just the clocks but her paintings and sculptures. Justin made sure to point out Courtney's work to everyone who came into the shop, and she beamed with pride at the positive feedback she received.

Days turned into weeks, and soon Courtney found herself painting more and more works on clocks and on canvas. With each new design, she gained more confidence in her abilities. Justin continued to support her, not just with his words but with small gifts and gestures that showed how proud he was of her.

Eventually, word got out about Courtney's art pieces, and more and more people started coming into the shop just to see her work. Sweetgum residents were particularly drawn to her designs and often asked her to create custom pieces for them.

It wasn't long before Courtney was approached by the local museum to create a series of works to showcase the town's history and aesthetic. She eagerly accepted the offer, and soon her work was on display for all to see.

As she stood in front of her art in the museum gallery, Courtney felt a sense of pride and accomplishment wash over her. Justin stood by her side, beaming with pride.

"You know," he said, "with all this success, you could open up your own art gallery."

Courtney's heart skipped a beat at the thought. In the past, she had never considered the idea of owning her own gallery, but now it seemed like a real possibility.

"You really think so?" she asked, looking up at him with hopeful eyes.

"Absolutely," he replied with a grin. "You're a natural talent, Courtney. I have no doubt that you could make it happen."

With Justin's encouragement, Courtney began to plan out her future. She knew it wouldn't be easy, but with dedication and support, she felt like anything was possible.

"YOU'RE GOING TO NEED THESE," Nevaeh chucked two tomatoes in Courtney's basket that morning. "The canned stuff doesn't taste authentic. If you blend those up and juice them, your pasta's going to taste like the real deal," she twisted her floppy hat so it flopped away from her forehead.

The soreness of Courtney's arms became apparent when she rested her goods on the market grounds. Was the Saturday market scene always this lively? Almost every face in town had come out to purchase fresh produce from farmers. The crowds buzzed with greetings, questions and comments as friends met up and farmers sold. Each stand attracted a great deal of customers, bringing smiles to many faces. The main path remained clear until customers crossed over to vendors nearby. One may label this scene chaotic but Courtney enjoyed it. A sense of community warmed her heart while watching people gather.

"Is he a fan of green onions?" Nevaeh picked up a handful from an old lady's stand. She waved it before Courtney for emphasis.

Courtney put Nevaeh's hand down. "He's a grown man who appreciates flavor, so yes," she asked for their pricing and was pleased with what she heard. "Alright, put them in Nev," she lifted her basket and Nevaeh dropped the seasoning. Courtney paid the kind old woman, then led the way forward.

Nevaeh's basket held carrots and potatoes for the soup she had in mind for lunch. She'd been low on those at her place, so she'd bought them while there. "What do you think he's going to say though?".

Courtney grew fluttery when the question was asked. "I don't know. It could be nothing. We've made dinner at his place a few times before. It's not every date that he makes some huge announcement. Sometimes we just enjoy each other's company. We're supposed to watch a movie afterward. He wants to congratulate me for my success." From the second he'd proposed that they dine at his house tonight, Courtney had been ecstatic about this meeting. It left her with a high that sped her heartbeat.

"You know Justin, Courtney. This isn't just about congratulating you. I think he has something else in mind. I mean… a lot's happened this week. It might have inspired him to get down on one knee—"

"Nevaeh!" Courtney whined when her friend snickered ruthlessly. Nevaeh buried her face in her shoulder to hide her theatrics. "You tease too much. It hasn't been that long. I mean yeah, we love each other but if he actually has some grand milestone to announce then it's probably something else," though she doubted that anything like that was in store. Again, they made dinner at his place all the time. Nevaeh's expectations were far too grand. "But anyway, help me pick out some thyme," she switched the hand she held her basket in, then turned down a different path.

Nevaeh followed quietly until she gasped. "Speak of the devil," she whispered to Courtney.

Courtney raised her head, only to be met by Justin. "Oh, hi," she smiled without thinking, then reached for a hug.

Justin held a basket of his own. He wasn't alone though. A tall well-built man with freshly cut hair stood beside him. He was Justin's best friend Sean who struck her as shy.

Courtney let go and pushed her hair from her face. "So, you're shopping for tonight too, huh?" she noticed the ingredients he carried. They were seasoning. Onions in particular. A few stray apples were in the mix.

"Yeah. For that and for the week," Justin waved at Nevaeh. "Are you her helper this morning Nevaeh?" he asked cheerily, eyes sparkling. Courtney was entranced by his heavenly appearance. The simple T-shirt and jeans were art on his body.

"You could say that," Nevaeh looked at Sean and waved a quick hello.

"Hey," Sean nodded his greeting. "You two seem to have a good thing going, so we're going to leave you. Courtney, you and Justin can exchange ingredients tonight, okay? How does that sound?" his tone seemed neutral compared to Justin's. He carried a pleasant attitude, though. It just paled in comparison to Justin's palpable excitement.

"Yes, yes. If we teamed up to shop, we'd never leave." Courtney joined Justin in a short laugh, her stomach filling with butterflies. "Anyway, I'll see you later, okay Justin?" she pressed her top teeth on her bottom lip, struggling to contain her growing anticipation.

"Of course," Justin kissed her cheek before leaving with Sean.

Nevaeh grabbed Courtney's arm. "Did you see how he looked at you? All smug-like? He has something to tell you. I know for sure now. There's no denying it," they gave room to passing marketgoers as they remained in place.

"Nevaeh you're crazy," Courtney pinched her friend's cheek, then told her to follow her. Her shopping list was far from complete.

JUSTIN WAS IN THE KITCHEN, finishing up dinner while Courtney tinkered with the music. As he plated the food, he thought about how lucky he was to have her in his life.

He set the plates down on the table and took a deep breath. "Courtney, can you come here for a second?" he called out.

She walked over to him, a curious expression on her face. "What's up?" she asked.

Justin smiled nervously, feeling his heart racing. "I have something to show you," he said, before disappearing into his room.

A few moments later, he emerged with a stack of canvases in

his hand. Courtney's eyes widened as he set them down on the table.

"What are these?" she asked, picking one up and examining it closely. "These are gorgeous! Did you paint these?"

Justin grinned. "They're paintings I did of us," he said. "I know I haven't really talked about it, but I love to paint. And I wanted to capture some of our special moments together."

Courtney looked at him in surprise, her eyes shining with emotion. "I had no idea you could paint," she said, a smile spreading across her face. "These are amazing, Justin. I can't believe you did all of this. I love this pop-art style."

He felt a warmth spreading through his chest as he watched her take in each painting. There were scenes of them laughing together, holding hands on a walk, and even one of her sitting alone, painting a clock.

"That one's my favorite," he said, pointing to the portrait of her. "I wanted to capture how beautiful you are, even when you're just doing everyday things. Also, no one knows that I like to paint. I've never shared that with anyone before, until now."

Courtney looked at him with tears in her eyes, touched by his words and the effort he had put into these paintings. "Thank you so much, Justin," she said, leaning over to kiss him. "You are so very talented, and I feel so honored that you would share this part of yourself with me. It seems it's another thing we have in common."

He wrapped his arms around her, feeling grateful for her presence in his life. This moment represented how much he had opened up to her and trusted her completely.

As they sat down to dinner, he knew that this was just the beginning of the beautiful things they would create together. Justin took a deep breath, his heart pounding in his chest as he looked across the table at Courtney. They had just finished making their enchanting one-pot pasta recipe, and everything seemed perfect - the soft sixties classics playing on the radio, the gentle glow of the candles, and the delicious smell of the pasta. He felt lucky to have her in his life and was thankful for every moment they spent together.

Justin had set the table with swan-shaped serviettes. He had spent hours perfecting his origami, and he was glad that Courtney appreciated his efforts. "I wanted everything to be perfect tonight," he said, watching her unfold the serviette and revealing the beautiful swan. "And I wanted to impress you with my origami skills."

"You did impress me," Courtney replied, grinning at him. "You're full of surprises."

Justin laughed, feeling a surge of happiness. "I try," he said, watching as Courtney took a bite of the pasta. "So, how is it?"

"It's amazing," Courtney replied, nodding her head. "You really outdid yourself this time."

Justin beamed, feeling proud of his cooking skills. He had always loved to cook, and it was one of the things that he and Courtney enjoyed doing together.

As they ate, the song 'Hey Jules' by the Beatles started playing on the radio, and Justin felt a sense of nostalgia wash over him. He loved the Beatles and had always been a fan of their music.

"Some songs never die," he said, tapping his foot to the beat. "And this is one of them."

"I know," Courtney replied, smiling at him. "It's a classic."

They finished their pasta, and Justin poured them each a glass of white wine. He smiled as he watched Courtney's eyes light up at the quality of the wine.

"You have exquisite taste," she said, taking a sip of her drink.

Justin chuckled, feeling pleased with himself. "I'm glad you like it," he said, taking a sip of his own wine. "I just want everything to be perfect for you."

Courtney put down her glass, twirling her hair, and turning

away from him. Justin knew that look—there was something important she needed to say.

"What is it?" he asked, concerned.

Courtney took a deep breath, meeting his gaze. "Justin, I just want to say that...I'm really happy with you," she said, her voice soft and sincere. "You make me feel so loved, and I don't know what I'd do without you."

Justin felt his heart swell with love for her. "I feel the same way," he said, taking her hand across the table. "You mean everything to me."

They sat there for a moment, holding hands and looking into each other's eyes. Justin knew that he wanted to spend the rest of his life with Courtney, but he also knew that they were not quite ready for marriage. Instead, he had another idea.

"Courtney, I know we're not quite ready for marriage yet," Justin said, pausing for a moment as he took a deep breath. "But I want to take our relationship to the next level. I want us to move in together."

Courtney's eyes widened in surprise, and Justin could feel his heart racing with anticipation. He waited for her response, hoping that she would feel the same way.

"I would love that," Courtney said, smiling at him. "I want to be with you, Justin."

Relief washed over him, and Justin felt like he could finally breathe again. "I'm so happy to hear that," he said, grinning from ear to ear.

Courtney stood up from her chair and walked around the table to hug him. Justin wrapped his arms around her, pulling her close to him. He could feel the warmth of her body against his, and he knew that this was where he belonged.

AUTHOR'S NOTE

Thank you so much for reading Infinite Kiss, the third book in the Sweetgum Meadows Romance series of stand-alone novels. I really hope you loved it! If you enjoyed this book, please consider leaving it a review so that others may also find it. Also, if you haven't read the first two books, yet, check them out today! Although these are stand-alone novels, the stories all intertwine and progress.

I look forward to introducing you to the other characters in this lovely, family-oriented town where each couple will find their happily ever after.

Would you like to receive bonus scenes and keep up with what's next with my upcoming books? Then, make sure you sign up for my mailing list on my website by visiting ImaniPrice.com.

ALSO BY IMANI PRICE

Book 1: Love Between Us

Book 2: Sweet Sunsets

Book 3: Infinite Kiss

Book 4: Dance With Me

Book 5: In Charge

Book 6: Forever With You

Book 7: Secret Sweethearts

Book 8: Endless Love

Book 9: The Harder We Fall

Book 10: Reservations of the Heart

Book 11: Play by Play

Book 12: Guarded Hearts

Book 13: Healing Hearts

Book 14: Dear Sweetgum

Book 15: Lanterns of the Meadows (novella)

Book 16: Drawn to You

Book 17: Under the Sweetgum Tree

Sweetgum Meadows' Visitor's Guide

To all my lovely readers,

Thank you
for
reading